Letters

from the

Inside

JOHN MARSDEN

Letters

from the

Inside

Houghton Mifflin Company
Boston 1994

Library of Congress Cataloging-in-Publication Data

Marsden, John, 1950-
    Letters from the inside / John Marsden. — 1st American ed.
      p.   cm.
    "Originally published in Australia in 1991 by Pan Macmillan
Australia Pty. Limited" — T.p. verso.
    Summary: The relationship between two teenage girls who become
acquainted through letters intensifies as their correspondence
reveals some of the terrible problems of their lives.
    ISBN 0-395-68985-6
    [1. Letters—Fiction. 2. Family problems—Fiction. 3. Emotional
problems—Fiction. 4. Friendship—Fiction. 5. Prisoners—Fiction.
6. Australia—Fiction.]   I. Title.
PZ7.M35145Le   1994   93-41185
[Fic]—dc20   CIP
                           AC

Printed in the United States of America
VB   10 9 8 7 6 5 4 3 2 1

ACKNOWLEDGEMENTS

Thanks for ideas and stories to:
Daniel Barrington-Higgs, Kyla Davies,
Marta Dusseldorp, Damien Morris,
Damien Nevine, Richard Wardill,
Michele Williams.

Special thanks to my "language consultant,"
the legendary Sam Armytage.

For Mary Edmonston

Letters

from the

Inside

Dear Tracey,

I don't know why I'm answering your ad, to be honest. It's not like I'm into pen pals, but it's a boring Sunday here, wet, everyone's out, and I thought it'd be something different.

Um, what do I say now? I know what I won't do, and that's tell you my star sign, favourite group, favourite food, all about my sister and brother and the usual junk. If that's what you want, don't bother answering this letter, OK? That's not me.

So, I'll just tell you whatever comes to mind, for example... um...

(1) The last time I cried was when I saw an old movie called *How Green Was My Valley*, in black and white at 2.30 in the morning last Monday, on Channel 7. I was a mess.

(2) Right now I've got $78.31 in the bank, $12.60 on me, my sister owes me $5.00, and a friend at school, Rebecca Slater, owes me $6.00. Total: $101.91.

(3) I'd love to get a tat, where no-one can see it, and it'd be of a cane toad, 'cos they're so cute, but I don't have the guts to do it.

(4) I've got a dog, or at least there's a dog who lives here with us. I don't think you can own an animal. He hasn't got a name, which drives everyone crazy. It's not that I'm against names, although I don't like them much. It's more that I can't think of a name for him. So everyone keeps suggesting names, like Toby (my sister), Onion???

(my friend Cheryl), Mick (my father) and Idiot (my brother).

He's only about a year old. He was dumped near the RSPCA shelter and we got him from there. He's nearly all white, with a bit of black round the head. I think he's a mix of Border Collie and twenty other things.

I was going to call him Gilligan, 'cos he's my little buddy, but it doesn't sound right.

Do any dogs or animals live with you?

Well, I've told you four things about myself, four amazing facts. And a lot more besides. And I've written a long letter. Hope you answer, after all this work! Bye!

Mandy

PS: How come you have a post-office box? I thought they were for big companies.

Feb 18

Dear Mandy,

Thanks for writing. You write so well, much better than me. I put the ad in for a joke, like a dare, and yours was the only good answer. There were three from guys, real perverts, pretty funny but disgusting. And a couple from little kids. It was exciting though, getting them all.

You asked if I have any pets, sorry, if any pets live with us. I have a horse, two dogs and a cat.

The horse is called Kizzy, the dogs are Dillon and Matt and the cat is Katie. So you see, they all have names. Why don't you like names?

You also asked why I gave a post-office box as the address. Well, that's my father's company. He owns a transport company, with lots of semi-trailers. They do mainly interstate work.

As for me, I'm in Year 10 but I hate school. The only good subject is Art. I play a lot of sport though, and I'm quite good at basketball and high jump. (I'm pretty tall, as you can guess.)

I don't know what else to tell you. I hope you keep writing though. It'd be fun writing letters to someone without ever meeting them. Prescott's a long way from Acacia Park. I've never been to Acacia Park or anywhere down that line. Does anyone read your letters or can I write anything I want?

Please write,
Tracey

≈

February 26

Dear Tracey,

What do you mean, does anybody read my letters? You must be joking. I'd nail them to the roll-a-door if they tried.

Well, I suppose my brother would if he could, or if he thought of it. It's OK though, he can hardly read as it is, so no problem.

3

It was quite exciting, getting your letter. I get about one letter a month. My grandmother writes occasionally, and a girl called Jacinta who I met at a writers' camp, and a boy who's at boarding school, a friend of a friend. So letters in my life are like sunflowers in Alaska.

I do write a lot of letters for Amnesty but not too many of those guys write back. Funny, that.

Was *G.D.Y.* the only magazine you put your ad in? Do you read *G.D.Y.* every month? Is that the only time you put an ad in? I'd love to see the letters you got from the dirty old men, or dirty young men, whichever they were. Send me some, OK? I still think it's funny I wrote to you, but I'm enjoying this. I read *G.D.Y.* most months but I'm too much of a tight-ass to buy it: I have a friend, Cheryl Tsang, who gets it, and I read hers.

S'pose I'd better tell you a few boring facts about myself. I'm in Year 10 at Acacia Park High. I'm 15, turning 16 on October 19. I've got a sister called Katrina — she's in first year arts at uni, and she's a good bird, more like a friend than a... blah blah blah... you know how it goes.

I've got a brother too, named Steve. He's 17.

Katrina's not living at home any more. She moved out at the start of last year, when she got accepted into uni. But then she deferred. She was waitressing at a Hungarian restaurant for about half the year, then she went overseas for a couple of months, then she came back and worked in pubs. She's still working in a pub three nights a week. It's the Stripes and Stars, in Sinden, if you ever

feel like a rage — just go there any Wednesday,
Thursday or Friday night, ask for Katrina, tell her
you're a mate of mine, and you should at least
get a free beer — and no ID! It's a definite advan-
tage having a sister in a job like that, although
my parents don't think so — they don't like her
working there.

God, this has turned into a long letter again. I've
written this instead of doing my homework. Better
stop and do Science at least. Oh help, just remembered there's a French test tomorrow! Gotta go.

Bye,
    Mandy

≈

Feb 28

Dear Mandy,

Thanks for your letter. Hope you passed your
French test. And thanks for the info about the
Stripes and Stars. Don't know whether I'll get there
though. My parents are pretty strict. They still like
us to do things together.

I've got an older sister and an older brother
too. My sister's name is Skye and my brother's
is Dean. My sister is 22 — she's a hairdresser and
my brother is 20 and studying to be a doctor. I'd
like to be a doctor. Actually I'd like to be a child-
ren's doctor, but I don't know if my marks will
be good enough.

5

My favourite activities, apart from sport, are water-skiing and horse-riding. And shopping. And raging. I like parties, pubs, discos, everything. And, don't laugh, but I like poetry too. Reading it and even writing it. I'm not very good at it, but I like it.

Yes, I do read *G.D.Y.* quite often. But that's the only time I've put an ad in. I know those magazines are pretty dumb. But they have some good stuff. I like the letters and the medical page!!! And the ads and some of the articles.

Do you like Dust and Ashes? I do. There was an article on them last month in *G.D.Y.* Do you know the drummer, Roy Lugarno? They said he'd been a street kid and got put in Ruxton for knocking off cars when he was 15. He's done well, hasn't he? You wouldn't think anyone could be such a star after two years in Ruxton.

You sound as though you don't like your brother much. What's wrong with him? My brother's good. I can talk to him about anything, and he's good when you've got problems. A lot of girls here don't get on with their brothers, but I'm lucky I guess.

Anyway, I haven't got anything interesting to write about, so I'll stop now. But write back, please.

Bye,
  Tracey

≈

Dear Trace,

Didn't get your letter till today, though you dated it Feb 28. What did you do, send it by rubber raft? Anyway, I'm answering straight away, so you'll know I'm still alive.

Everything's quite slack at the moment. I've got some slack teachers this year, in English and History anyway. Maths and French we get heaps of work, and Science, some. I've been trying to figure out how to earn money. Got any ideas? I made a bit in the holidays, working Friday nights and Saturday mornings at Safeway, plus I babysat quite a lot, but God, I spend money as fast as I earn it. Cheryl and Rebecca and I are going to the Power Without Glory concert Saturday week; then I bought their new CD yesterday, *Confessions*, that's about fifty bucks all up, just on Power Without Glory. Hope they're grateful.

What else is happening in my exciting life? I got 56% in that French test by the way, which is as bad as a fail, seeing nearly everyone else got in the seventies or better.

Here's Cheryl:

Hi Tracey!

Mandy told me how she started writing to you and how you've been writing back! I think it's great! I love getting letters! Do you go to Prescott High? I've never been over there. How's your love life? Get Mandy to tell you about *Paul*! He likes her but she can't make up her mind. Tell her to get with him, OK? Bye for now!

Cheryl Tsang

Ignore all the above — Cheryl's going through menopause or something. Paul is Paul Bazzani, who is nice but I don't know if he likes me. Cheryl's lusting after Paul's brother, Mick, who's in Year 12 — that's the real reason she wants me to get with Paul.

You asked about my brother — yeah, he's a creep. I mean, he's creepy. It's bad at the moment, with Katrina not living at home and my parents working day and night, night and day. I'm at home with my brother more than I'd like.

Oh well, better wind up. We're in the library — it's been another slack lesson. We've got Mr Prideaux for Geography and every lesson he either shows a video or we have a library period. Yesterday we had three videos — in English, Geography and Art. Might as well stay home and watch TV.

Gotta go, everyone's packing up. See you!

Mandy

≈

Dear Mandy,

Sorry my letters take so long to get to you. Guess I keep forgetting to post them.

I've been out riding my horse. He's so nice, with such trusting eyes. He comes to the fence every time he sees me and stands there nibbling my shirt while I stroke him and scratch him. He's getting a bit fat though, so I gave him a good long work-out.

My parents drive me to gymkhanas at weekends. They like doing it and they say they're proud of me, 'cos I've won quite a few ribbons and trophies. It's hard, but it's worth it. I'd love to ride at the Olympics or something like that.

How's it going with Paul? He sounds nice — I think you should go for it! I've been with my boyfriend for three months — his name's Casey Winter — he's gorgeous looking and really kind and loving but I don't know how much longer to keep it going. Three months is a long time! I don't want it to get too serious, although he does.

I don't know what to suggest about earning money. My parents give me heaps of pocket money, plus they pay for my clothes and everything — my father says he wants me to look nice. So I don't need much money.

I'm still curious about your brother. How come he's creepy? What does he do, try to crack onto you or something?

Bad luck about your French, though I'd say 56% was pretty good. Better than I'd ever get.

Well, Mum's just called out to say dinner's ready, so I'd better go. It's really nice tonight — she's cooked Hawaiian Chicken, my favourite. And she doesn't like us to be late.

Bye!
Tracey

PS: Say 'hi' to Cheryl for me, and thanks for the note.

≈

March 17

Dear Trace,

Geez, your life sounds perfect. Great family, great boyfriend, stacks of money. I'm jealous! You want to swap?

What school do you go to anyway? In one letter you said something that sounded like a boarding school. But I guess not, or you would have mentioned it. And what are you doing for Easter? Slipping over to New York for a few days?! It'd be funny if you were coming up this way and we could meet! Wonder if we will, eventually.

I'm writing this at eleven o'clock at night — well it's nearly midnight now — in front of TV, while I pig out on biscuits and chips and grapes. 'Rage' has just come on.

Speaking of rage, that's what I was meant to be doing tonight but thanks to the lovely Paul Bazzani, it didn't work out. Actually, it's been a

10

fart of an evening. You see, I was meant to be going with Paul to this party, at Marco Tanimides' place. That was OK, we got there all right (Paul paid for a taxi), but it was a bit of a set-up if you ask me. There were only eight people there and I didn't know any of them. I mean they were from school but they're not the people I hang round with. Some of them I didn't even know their names. They were off their faces by the time we got there, and they were into everything, there were condoms flashing around and people disappearing into the bushes in the backyard. And I don't even know Paul that well: like, this was the first time I'd gone anywhere with him. It was a set-up for sure.

Anyway, without going into the gory details, it ended with Paul calling me frigid and all that, and me walking home, about a hundred ks on my own. And I tell you, I was scared. It gets pretty rough around Acacia Park on a Saturday night. And to make matters worse, I knew no-one was home here.

Oh well, I survived. But I'm so burned off. I thought Paul was OK actually. Wait till I see Marco on Monday, I'll kill him. In fact I think I'll ring him tomorrow.

Wonder what you're doing right now. Probably at the ballet or opera or something. Sorry, I'm heaping it on you. It's the mood I'm in. Blame Paul. Anyway, I can't be bothered writing any more — think I'll go to bed and continue this later.

Power Without Glory's next Saturday. Hope it's an improvement on this weekend. At least it's something to look forward to. Write me back a great letter, make my week, OK?

Sweet dreams
Mandy

≈

Mar 20

Dear Mandy,

I don't know what I said that sounded like a boarding school. I must have been dreaming. Don't you ever do that? Write things that are totally wrong, when you're half-asleep or thinking about something else? I do it all the time. Or maybe you just misunderstood me. Trouble is, I don't remember what I said.

Anyhow, I go to Prescott High, though not many people know me there because I'm so quiet.

Your weekend must have been a real winner. What's happened since? Paul sounds like a con-artist. What's he look like? You better watch out for him!

Casey and I went to a party too, at Ruyton Heads. One of his mates has a beach house there and his parents let him have it for the weekend. It was some party! Spin out! But I can trust Casey.

I did get a bit wasted though. We had cans of UDL, gin and tonic, and I guess I had more than I thought. So I ended up in a mess and felt sick and disgusting all day Sunday. It was worth it though.

But my life's not as perfect as you think.

How's your dog? Have you got a name for him yet? You could call him Roy, after Roy Lugarno from Dust and Ashes. Or call him something so dumb and obvious that it's funny, like Rover or Spot or Lassie. I used to like *Harry the Dirty Dog*. You ever read that book? Don't know why I didn't call my dog Harry.

Next Saturday while you're raging at the Power Without Glory concert I've got our big basketball game. If we win this we end up second in the minor premiership and go into the major semi. If we lose we'd probably only come fourth or fifth — it depends on the other results. So this week is solid training. Basketball's a good game though — I like it. Today we were doing bounce passes and rebounds, plus working out some new signals. Trouble is, Mrs Strauss, she's our coach, I don't think she knows as much as some of the players. And she tries to be popular by giving us slack work-outs but most of us would rather go for it...

Anyway, I'm just raving on. Hope life's cool, and that you've sorted out Paul and Marco.

Bye,
    Trace

≈

Dear Trace,

God, that's a boring way to start a letter. I'll come up with something better next time, I promise. But my life's boring at the moment. Can't wait till the holidays, not that we're doing anything or going anywhere. Oh well. At least the Power Without Glory concert was good. Actually it was better than good; it was over the mountain and far away. It was a great great concert. I didn't go with anyone, any guys I mean, just Cheryl and Rebecca, but that was fine by me. Sisters of Rock were the support band and I like them, too.

That Phil Nuffield, he's amazing. He was jumping off the stage into the audience and jumping back up again and ripping off these amazing vocals through it all. There were four encores so it went late. Those encores are a pain in the butt — the bands know they're going to play them, they've rehearsed them and everything, the crowd know they're going to play them — but you've still got to go though the routine of clapping till your hands are burning. It's so fake.

Anyway, I'm being selfish, 'cos Saturday was your big basketball game. How did you go? Did you win? Hope so. I actually remembered it a few times during the night and crossed my fingers for you — maybe it was when you were shooting the winning goal.

You know, that's — don't take this the wrong way — but that's one of the first times since we've been writing that you've let yourself go a bit, like it was the 'real you' or whatever you want to call it.

You seem reserved. Is that what you're like in real life? I keep thinking of questions I want to ask you but it's hard when you're a week away. For instance, who are your friends? (apart from Casey). What do you look like? Send me a photo. Do you believe in God? Do you do drugs? Do you smoke? Do you get on with everyone in your family? Do you follow a footy team? Are you a brain at school? What kind of jokes make you laugh? What kind of clothes do you wear? Gee, now that I've started, I could go on all night. Lucky I don't have to answer these questions myself. Have you ever been anywhere, like travelling?

Sorry if I'm overdoing it! You don't have to answer them anyway.

Oh yes, I was going to tell you about Paul and Marco. Well believe me, I'm offering this as a script to 'Days of Our Lives'. But I handled it good! I handled it great! I've never been this tough before! I rang Marco Sunday night and just blew him off the phone. Poor guy, he didn't know what hit him. You see, I'd had all day (and a lot of Saturday night) to think about what I wanted to say. I was right though — he virtually admitted Paul had asked him to get a few people together and have a 'party' because he wanted to screw me. Bastards.

Well, Monday morning I walked right past Paul like I was the principal of the school. I treated him like scum all day, even though he tried to talk a few times. But after school I let him have it, face to face. And not the kind of face to face he'd been hoping for Saturday night. I told him how I'd trusted him and thought he was a pretty straight guy and how much I'd changed my mind about him. He just stood there dripping with guilt. And he grovelled for a long time. Actually we parted on OK terms. You know, I don't mind him — he's a decent guy, but he hangs around with some of life's legendary losers.

So, that all happened yesterday, though it seems a long time ago. Today was good. Paul was ultra-nice all day and Marco avoided me. But best of all, I'm proud of myself for putting it to them like that!

Good luck in the finals, if you're in them!

Love,
Mandy

≈

Mar 29

Dear Mandy,

Thanks for your letter. I don't know how to answer your letters sometimes. What to say to you. You say I seem quiet and reserved. Well maybe I am. But you seem confident. Is that what you're like in real life? The way you dealt with those guys, that was good.

I get the feeling that if we met we probably

16

wouldn't even be friends. If we went to the same school for instance.

Well, we took the basketball game, 54–50. It wasn't one of our best efforts, but we won. Day after tomorrow's the first final — if we take that we go straight to the grand final. I'm nervous already, to tell you the truth. It's against a team called Chieftains who've beaten us twice this season. Last time they thrashed us but that was the worst we've played. (Our best player had suddenly left so we were a bit of a mess.)

We had training this afternoon — I've just come in, had a shower and sat down to write this letter. It was a hard training for once — our captain, a girl called Kylie Patrick, ran it, and Mrs Strauss let her. Kylie knows more about basketball than Mrs Strauss anyhow. So it was good. I like it better when it's hard, even though during it you're thinking, 'I hate it, I wish it was over.'

I keep coming back to your letter. I'm not sure what to think when you talk about 'the real me'. I thought I was writing about the real me. But I'll try to answer your questions.

What do I look like? Well, I'm tall (176 cm) and I think I'm overweight, although everyone else says I'm just being anorexic. Wish I did have anorexia sometimes (though I've seen a few girls with it, and it's pretty off). I'm blonde, my hair's long at the moment, I've got blue eyes, fair skin (burns easily), have a modelling contract already signed — as if.

I don't believe in God, definitely not.

I don't do drugs or smoke, don't drink or talk to strange men. Actually I sink the odd can or two and I wouldn't mind talking to some strange men if I could find any.

I get on with everyone in the family — we're close, like I told you. I can talk to my parents about anything and they're really proud of us. So many kids' parents get divorced, but mine have been married twenty-five years, and they never argue or anything.

I don't follow footy much but I go for Norths. (Mainly because of Sam Marcroftsis, he's so cute. He reminds me of my brother.)

I'm not a brain at school but I do OK.

What kind of jokes make me laugh? Well, here's the latest:

Q. What do you call a fly with no wings?
A. A walk.

Pretty funny, hey?! Oh well, I thought it was.

What kind of clothes do I wear? I don't like to dress up, although my father likes me to. He always wants me to wear expensive skirts and stuff, but I'm happy with jeans and a top. Those American sweatshirts, for example: I've got a few of those. I like clothes by Daniel, Heresy, Double First. I wear quite a bit of jewellery. I guess I do like some expensive things.

And for your final question: We went overseas, to Disneyland and Hawaii and London, when I was little, but I don't remember much about it.

Now I'll ask you some questions. What kind

of stuff do you do with your friends? What's your room like? Is it your own or do you share? What do you look like? Send me a photo. (Sorry I haven't got any of me that I like.) Why's your brother creepy? (You never answer that one.) How strict are your parents? Do you believe in God?

You see, you're getting a taste of your own medicine now.

I'm so jumpy tonight. I think it's that basketball. I'm all over the place, been having fights and getting in trouble, can't do any work. Wish Casey was here to hold me and press against me and run his fingers down my back. God I love that guy. But he's training tonight — he's so fit. Well, I might go and play some music — Nicotine Monsters, I think. That's the mood I'm in.

Wish me luck! See you!

Tracey

≈

Mar 31

Mandy!

WE WON! I can't believe it! By seven points! I'm so excited I had to tell someone, and you're it. I mean nobody, just nobody, beats Chieftains. And I played OK too — sixteen points, second highest, and some good rebounds. Got fouled off in the last two minutes, but who gives? It's so great — hope we can keep our heads on till the Grand Final.

Oh well, gotta go to bed. But it's so exciting, I wanted to tell you.

Love, *Trace*

≈

Dear Trace,

Wow, you star! That's fantastic! I'm rapt. Congratulations. I've never done anything like that in my life. So when's the big one? Bet you're revved-up for it. That's a hot team you've got there. Better tell Mrs Strauss to get herself in gear.

I love basketball — well, watching it I mean. I've been to a couple of NBL games and they were great — the atmosphere was huge. And I watch it on TV sometimes. I love those American guys. I wish I was tall and black and cool. Instead I'm short and pinky-brown and not cool enough.

So have you stopped celebrating yet? Wonder if you'll be playing Chieftains again in the Grand Final. If you do you should be confident.

This has been a good couple of days, a good start to the week. Katrina was home for the weekend, and stayed till last night (think she missed a few classes). It's so good when she's home — everything's much better. Plus I scored a heavy 78% in a Maths test, which is good for me, especially as we were doing parabolas, which I hate. I can't see the use of them.

You sure turned the tables on me with those questions. They're good though — they made me think. Some are a bit hard to answer, like, what my friends and I do in our spare time. I mean, we just do all the obvious stuff, like goss, back-stab, shop, go to the movies, check out guys, talk on the phone, play music. We even do homework once in a while. Cheryl Tsang, who wrote you that note, lives round the corner from me, and Rebecca Slater's three blocks away, and Maria Kagiasis is opposite her. They're about my best mates.

We're into sport a bit too. Maria and Rebecca and I are in the same softball team, called Mum's Army ('cos Maria's mum coaches us). But it's pretty low-key, and we don't do that well. Maria's a mean hitter though.

Well, next question. My room's a complete mess, now and forever. It has a bed, but not much else that anyone'd recognize. There are clothes everywhere, probably more of Cheryl's and my sister's than mine. But if it was ever neat (you have to use a lot of imagination here) you'd see something like this: a bed with a doona cover of sheep playing in a paddock in cute little ways; a desk under the window, covered with books; a set of shelves with more books and ornaments and toys; a dressing-table with more ornaments and family and school photos; and a built-in wardrobe with posters on the doors (mainly of Power Without Glory, needless to say).

The curtains are old white lace ones that used

to be in my grandmother's house. On the wall are a couple of pictures: one of my grandparents standing next to their first car; then a painting called *Science and Charity*, by Picasso; and then one of the ocean, by a guy called Christopher Pratt. I was allowed to choose them myself.

As for my brother, I'll tell you about him another time, when I'm not in such a good mood. I don't want to spoil this letter.

OK, last two questions. Well, for one, my parents aren't bad. They're strict on some things, like money, but Katrina softened them up on important issues like parties and curfews — and tidy rooms. They work hard, so they're not home as much as some parents. They get in late quite often.

And yes, I believe in God, although not the way the churches talk about Him/Her. I think that there's something there, some force, some presence. We had this guy who took us for religion last year. He said he was an atheist until one day in Wales, when a friend took him to the top of a mountain, pointed to the view and said, 'Now tell me there's no God'. And the guy fell to his knees and was converted. I'm a bit like that I guess. I can't look at a sunset or the sky at night or my dog or a Pizza Supreme and not believe in God.

Wow, I'm exhausted by this letter. But why is writing a long letter to you so easy, and a 300-word English essay so hard? God knows. I wonder if She/He does. Anyway, good luck for the big game, keep in training: don't smoke, drink or the other thing — see you —

Love,
Mandy

≈

Dear Mandy,

Thanks for your letter. If I fall asleep before I finish this paragraph, hope you forgive me. What with training and schoolwork and everything else I'm out of it. But I liked your letter. I knew you'd understand how I felt about the basketball.

There's nothing much to write about, so this could be short. My brother Dean was here for the weekend, and he came to our game, and took the whole team to McDonalds afterwards. We had a great time. It was so nice of him. He went back to university yesterday.

Next Friday's a black one, the 13th. Our game's the next day. Hope it's not an omen.

I'm going shopping tomorrow, mainly for new jeans. I had some really good ones — light blue Geminis — but when I was feeding the horse yesterday they caught on a nail and ripped open, down the leg. It's so annoying. Guess I shouldn't have been wearing them to feed the horses. Hurt my leg too, scratched it deep, but not enough to need stitches.

Then tomorrow night I'm going to a party with Casey, at a friend's of his. Some huge place, with a swimming pool and spa and everything. Should be fun. Hope Casey behaves himself. But I'll forgive him if he doesn't.

I'm too tired to write any more. Night!

Love,
Tracey

April 12

Dear Trace,

One week of school to go. I can hardly wait. This term seems to have taken forever. And generally it's sucked.

I'm feeling so down and out. There's too much work at school. Most of the teachers are stuffed. I can't keep up with French. Rebecca's being a bitch. This is definitely one of those weeks, one of those years, one of those lifetimes.

Rebecca's got it in for me at the moment. She's such a back-stabber. Every time I make a comment she says something sarcastic, and God help me if I crack a joke. It's all those little things — like, if we're in a class with Helen and Cheryl, she'll keep seats for all of us, but if it's only Rebecca and me she doesn't keep a seat. She makes me so mad! We went right through primary school together, and she's always been hot and cold.

So what are you doing for these holidays? Something glamorous and exciting with your perfect family? Sorry, I'm getting like Rebecca. But I hope you realize how lucky you are. Anyway, I think I've asked you about your holidays before. But I don't think you answered.

I met a girl from Prescott High yesterday, but she didn't know you. Anthea or Athina or some name like that. She's in Year 11. She's an exchange student from Greece, and they had a meeting here. We've got two Greek ones; one of them's in some of my classes, a guy called Phil. He seems nice but I haven't had much chance to get to know him.

Maybe while I'm feeling so bad I ought to answer your questions about my brother. I keep putting it off because I don't want to poison these letters, but this one's sour already. So... Steve. Where do I start? Bloody Steve. I gotta tell you Trace, this isn't easy. Something in my head is telling my arm not to write any more. But I'll probably keep going, now that I've started.

See, Trace, the trouble is, I'm scared of Steve. Scared of my own brother — it's not meant to be like that, is it? But Steve is a violent guy. I mean really violent, seriously violent. He's still at school, in Year 12, except I don't think he does any work. But the worst thing is, no-one seems to realize how bad he is, except me. It's not just that he's got a bad temper, though he sure has that. It's not just that his room's full of Rambo posters, that he watches all these violent movies, that he dresses in Army greens, or that he's got all kinds of weapons, like two old guns of Grandpa's and butterfly knives and nunchaku and Rambo knives. Those things alone wouldn't worry me, although I'd think anyone was a bit of a nerd if they were the biggest thrills in his life. But it's more than that. When Steve gets mad — and you never know what's likely to make him mad, it can be any little thing — the only way he ever reacts is violently. It's like, he doesn't know any other way. And he goes cold — his eyes go dead, you can't talk to him, his face goes blank and his voice is like a robot. I don't know whether he does it to look and sound tough, or whether it's a part of him that he can't control, but whichever it is, I know its effect on me, and that's bad.

He's beaten me up sometimes. Not like I've got any black eyes or broken bones, but he's hurt me. He's bent my fingers back, bent my arm back, kneed me, kicked me in the crutch, all kinds of stuff. And it's always when no-one's around. He's smart like that. I get so scared when I know the two of us are going to be home alone. That's one reason I hated it when Katrina left.

And when I've tried to talk to my parents they brush it off. It's like they don't want to face it. When I complain (and it's dangerous to complain when Steve's around) they tell me not to provoke him, just to ignore it, that I must be exaggerating, or that he's 'going through a stage', or they say 'Well that's what boys are like.' I think the guy's got a problem, but how do I convince Mum and Dad?

Katrina doesn't think he's that bad, 'cos she was bigger and stronger than him when they were growing up, and he's always been scared of her. And I don't like to talk to my friends about it, although they do think he's weird. For that matter, no-one likes him much — he's got no real friends, just a couple of other losers who are into the same kind of Rambo stuff. But they're not as bad as him. What I can't work out is how Mum and Dad keep ignoring his reports from school, because the school's complained about him a few times, and he got suspended last year for bullying. All his reports say he's got a terrible temper and he has to learn to control it. But he hasn't learnt, and I don't think he will.

You know, I read about those guys who do things like the Richmond Park killings, and the Harvey House Massacre, and I wonder if that's how my own brother will end up. That's not too good, is it?

Well, this must be the longest letter I've ever written. Hope you're awake. Sorry it's been so depressing. But now you know why I think you're lucky. Don't throw away what you've got, Trace, 'cos it's worth a rainforest, having a family like yours.

I'm going to crawl off to bed. It's after midnight — I'm too tired even to slash my wrists — I'll have to do it tomorrow.

See you — lots of love,
Mandy

≈

Dear Mandy,

Well, yesterday was the big one, and we lost. Bloody hell, I hate losing. I hate it, I hate it, I hate it. We played Chieftains again and they thrashed us, 60–36. But it was a bloody rough game. They got away with everything under the sun. See, the refs in our comp, they hate our guts, so we're always playing against seven people. I got fouled off three minutes into the second half, and I reckon one of the fouls was fair enough — all the others were total rip-offs. I'm still steaming. I mean, I'm bloody bruises from head to foot but I'm the one who got fouled. It sucks, it absolutely sucks.

Chieftains were so up themselves after the game. I'd rather any team in the comp but them won it. They were so psyched-up from the semi, it was like playing a football team.

We had a party afterwards but it was a dumb party. Now I'm watching *Video Super Hits*. I hate that Wave song, 'Lovers and Strangers', don't you? I've seen it a million times.

You asked about the holidays, but we're not doing anything. Dad says we've had too many trips lately and we should stay at home and have a family time. I don't mind.

That girl you met from Prescott, I don't know who she is. We don't mix with the Year 11s much. And anyway, like I told you, I'm quiet, so not many people know me.

Anyhow, I've got a History test tomorrow, better go and study.

Bye,
Tracey

≈

April 17

Tracey, how can you ignore my letter like that? I mean, it's bad about your basketball but I told you stuff about Steve that I've never told anyone, and you didn't say a word about it!

I was waiting for your letter, and when it came, all it had was bloody basketball. In fact I started thinking maybe you hadn't got my one, but you mentioned the exchange student, so you must have. I can't believe it.

Love (but burned-off),
Mandy

≈

Apr 20

Dear Mandy,

I'm sorry about your letter and your brother and everything. I knew you'd be pissed. But I didn't know what to say. I still don't know what to say.

When I put that ad in, and you answered, I thought you were such a funny and lively person, and sort of casual, happy-go-lucky. All the things that I'm not, to tell you the truth. Those comments you made once in a while about your brother, when you said he was a creep or something, I just thought he was lazy or selfish or a lagger. I didn't know there was anything serious. Then your letter came and I read it. I felt a bit sick. I thought, 'God, she's got problems like everyone else.' I don't think I wanted to know that.

What I can't understand is, how come you put it to those guys who tried to crack onto you, Paul and the other one, how come you put it to them with so much spunk, but your brother's got it all over you? I thought you were bloody tough the way you went after Paul. I can't work it out.

Guess you're on holidays now. I know I told you we're not going anywhere, but are you? Hope you haven't shot through, or you won't be getting this for a while. Not that it's worth getting anyway.

Sorry,
    Tracey

≈

April 26

Dear Trace,

Well, thanks for writing back. I don't blame you for being confused — I confuse myself sometimes.

Maybe I shouldn't have written to you the way I did. But I had to talk to someone. And these letters, it's funny, they're different. It's a different type of friendship. In a way I hope we never meet — it might spoil it. Somehow these letters are like a diary, and I write things in them that are different to the way I talk to people I see every day. So if we meet, or when we meet, it's like we'll have to start one type of friendship when we've already got another one. It's like we'd be starting from scratch when we'd already been going a hundred years. I don't know how it'd work.

I don't know whether I'm funny and lively, like you say, but I like a laugh and I do some radical things. But I'm not casual, or slack. Maybe in these letters I make myself out to be more of a social star than I am. You can do that in letters. After all, what you know about me is what I choose to tell you — I could be making it all up.

Sometimes when I write to you it's like I'm writing to myself.

I've been thinking about who sees the true side of me, because everyone sees different ones: my parents, my sister, my brother, Cheryl, Rebecca, Maria, you, the bus driver, my French teacher... But they're all true in their different ways (all fake too, sometimes). Guess it shows how many sides we all have. You know how people insult each other by saying they're 'two-faced'? The reason it's an insult is because it's an understatement! I'm thousand-faced.

Your letter only came today, thanks to Easter and Anzac Day. It's been a scungy holiday so far. I hate it when all the shops are shut. Sunday we went to church, not a common event in our family. My mother's always at us to go to confession and mass. She goes quite often but Dad's not even Catholic. He went on Easter Sunday though, so did Steve. Now if anyone should go to confession it's Steve, but the priests would have to sit in relays.

Katrina wasn't there but she came home afterwards and we had a proper big-time Easter dinner, with turkey. We're too old to have an egg hunt but we still got the eggs. I kind of miss the old egg hunts, to tell you the truth.

Uncle Kevin and Auntie Sophie came, with Justin, who's their only son. Uncle Kevin is Dad's twin brother and Justin is 18 and doing dentistry. He's a fun guy, the kind of sweetheart who passes his time by coughing up big gobs and spitting them at the rubbish tin. Too bad if you're walking past at the time, like I was when I stayed with them once. He should make a great dentist.

Yesterday I went into town with Cheryl. We didn't exactly plan it, but we ended up watching the parade of the old diggers. It was amazing. Actually it was sad, seeing them march along. The saddest thing was to see the World War One guys. There'd be a sign saying Second Division, and behind it there'd be three or four men, and you'd think, 'Once there would have been thousands, maybe tens of thousands, walking behind that banner, and now there's only three left, in their nineties, representing those fit young guys.' It seemed so tragic. And the World War Two ones were starting to look old and slow too.

32

My father was too young for World War Two and too old for Vietnam, so he was lucky. But both my grandfathers were in it, one in the army and one in the air force.

But the worst thing was after the parade. Cheryl and I were walking along Mortimer Avenue. This was about four o'clock in the afternoon. These guys were coming towards us, in their suits with medals and ribbons all over them. They were from the Vietnam war I guess, and they were drunk. Anyway, when they saw Cheryl — she's Malaysian — they started yelling out stuff like 'Get the gook! Get the gook!' and they fanned across the footpath making machine-gun noises and acting like they had guns. They thought they were being funny, but Jesus it was so bad. Cheryl just burned red, but I tell you, that girl's got guts. She walked right through them, without looking at them, without slowing down or speeding up. And tough old me — you remember how you said I was tough? — I tagged along behind her hoping to God they wouldn't touch us and there wouldn't be any trouble. Well we got away, but we didn't get away really. I think it left a mark or two.

Cheryl's got one thing in common with you though. She wouldn't talk about it — not one damn word.

Maybe the world's full of Steves. Maybe Steve's the man of the future, and in a few more years the world will be run by Steves.

Now that Easter and Anzac Day are over it's going to be two weeks here of Steve and me, me and Steve. And if you don't think I feel sick at that idea, you don't know me too well.

So, have a good holiday Trace!

Love,
Mandy

≈

Apr 27

Dear Trace,

Sorry about the letter I sent this morning. I was burned-off at everyone and everything, like I've been a lot lately. I can't remember exactly what I wrote, but think it was a bit depressing and sarcastic. So, sorry.

Today's been good actually. Steve went to town about ten o'clock and he isn't back yet. Mum and Dad'll be late. So I've had a peaceful day, doing nothing. Rebecca rang up for a goss and talked for an hour and a half — the rest of the time I've been reading this great great book, *Bound for Glory*. Do you know it? It's amazing. By Woodie Guthrie.

Anyway, I won't rave on like I normally do. I just wanted to tell you to ignore any bits in the last letter where I sounded more raggy than usual — as far as you were concerned, anyway.

Hey listen, here's a good idea! Why don't you ring me? 762398. Or is that a good idea? Maybe we should keep it at letters. Anyway, you decide!

Take care,
Mandy

≈

Dear Mandy,

Both your letters came in the same mail so it was OK — I didn't mind. Anyhow, you hadn't said anything that bad.

We got back yesterday actually. Dad had this sudden thing that he wanted to go to Porpoise Beach, so off we went. Skye and Dean managed to get away too, so the whole family was there.

I was going to send you a postcard but I forgot to take your address, and I couldn't remember if it was 438 or 348. I should remember, after all this time.

Anyhow, we had a great holiday. It only rained one afternoon. There was a heated pool at the hotel and I hung out in that nearly every day. Met this incredible hunk called Greg. Talk about a stud — he goes in ironman events, and he was an ironman all right, in more ways than one. The rest of the time he works as a lifesaver at the pool. He's a lot older than me but I don't care, even though my parents weren't too happy.

Greg's father had a Porsche and Greg borrowed it to take me out. We went to restaurants and nightclubs and everything — it was ace. You feel so good riding in those things. People look at you as if you're really someone.

I packed on a few ks, but it was worth it. We pigged out every day, on crayfish and prawns and steaks and pizzas — it's the best I've eaten in my life.

Greg is a special guy — caring and gentle, but strong too. He's already rung since we got back, and I'm hoping he'll come down in a few months. Or maybe I'll go up there again.

Don't know what'll happen with Casey. I don't want to tell him about Greg — hope he doesn't find out. The thing is, I like them both. They're both so nice, and good-looking. Greg's one of those guys, like that golfer, I can't remember his name, big and blond, all muscle. Casey looks like James Morrison — you like the Doors? — so they're different to each other. But I know every girl who sees them is jealous of me.

So, hope your holidays are going well, and that Steve's behaving himself. We're not doing much else, but I'd better do a bit of riding the next few days — my horse has put on a few ks too, plus I need the practice.

See you!
    Love,
        Tracey

≈

May 4

Dear Trace,

Thank God it's Friday, that's all I can say. Good name for a movie, hey? Actually, it's a bad name for a movie — it was the worst movie I've ever seen.

Anyway, the best thing about today is that it's

the last weekday of the holidays. I never thought I'd be glad to see a holiday end, but I've learnt a few things. And although there's still Saturday and Sunday to go, Mum and Dad'll be home both days.

Even though you obviously don't want to know about Steve, all I can say is tough titties. There's nobody else I can talk to — well, there's people I can talk to but I don't want to. It's safer writing to you, because I don't have to look at any faces and see the expressions — embarrassment, mostly. And I don't have to listen to their meaningless replies: 'You've been watching too many movies.' ... 'You've got too much imagination Mandy.' 'He's not that bad.' 'Just keep away from him.' 'Lock your door.'

Really helpful. Thanks a lot guys.

No, I know some of them, especially Cheryl, do try. They believe me. But they don't know what to say that would be any help. And they're right of course. What can they say? Words aren't going to solve anything.

Maybe you feel the same — maybe that's why you don't say much about Steve in your letters.

Anyway, the last week has been terrible. The first few days were OK — we stayed out of each other's path. At the weekend we had a fight over something so pathetic I'm embarrassed — no, I'll tell you, because right from the start I've been determined to be honest with you. There were two cans of drink left in the fridge, one Diet Coke and one Sarsparilla. And, you guessed it, we both wanted the Diet Coke. Pathetic, hey? Well, I got the Coke, because Mum intervened, but it was one of those victories, what are they called? where you win but you wish you hadn't. As Steve burned off to his room, kicking furniture and slamming doors, he muttered 'You wait' at me, which ruined my sleep for the rest of the weekend.

Sunday he kept trying to pick me all day, but with Mum and Dad around it was like the top was still on the bottle. Monday was the same, only worse — you've got no idea how bad he can be. If he wants something, it's like 'Come here slut,' or, 'Get me a sandwich, bitch.' If I'm feeling brave, or stupid, I'll say 'Get it yourself'; if I'm feeling weak but smart, I do it.

Tuesday I went to *T.C. and Me*, with Maria Kagiasis, and a friend of hers, a girl called Sophie. It's not a bad movie. Have you seen it? I don't usually like Trent Smith but the part suits him. And I love Jean Rawicz — I've seen every movie she's made.

Wednesday. Yes, well, Wednesday. We've got this computer game called 'Rum Jungle', OK? It was a Christmas present, and not a bad one. And although I'm not into computers much, I've been playing this one a bit and doing well (top score 12 660). Well, Wednesday morning Steve decided he'd have a go. It took all of ten minutes for him to start steaming. When he got into swearing, hitting the computer and kicking it, I went over and stood behind him. Like an idiot I thought that if I gave him a clue or two, he mightn't get so mad, and that way I could save the disc, the computer and me. And he might even get some satisfaction from posting a high score. OK, I know it was dumb, but that's what I thought. See I made the mistake of treating him like a normal person for once.

It didn't take long to work out what he was doing wrong. Or one thing he was doing wrong. So I said, 'You have to get that green one, and that slows down the yellow ones.' No reaction. A minute later the green thing appeared again, Steve deliberately ignored it, the yellow ones started accelerating, and five seconds later they wiped him out.

For that I got hit twice in the face and twice in the tits, a whole lot of computer stuff got hurled across the room, and Steve took all the discs so I couldn't use the computer. Plus a threat: 'Try lagging on me this time bitch, and I'll get you at school again.'

That's the trouble, see. Last year I lagged on him, and a few days later someone crapped in my bag, during recess at school. Now how do I prove it was him? I can't, but I know it was, from things he said to me — little hints and sick jokes.

Yesterday and today were average — I got a dead-leg about an hour ago for disagreeing with him about a TV show.

What I can't stand is the tension. Even if he's been quiet for days it doesn't mean anything. I can't relax when he's in the house.

When I write about him in these letters I go

out and post them straight away. Ever since you asked about people reading my mail. It'd be terrible if he knew I was telling you about it.

So, that's the story of my holidays. Not quite Porpoise Beach, but there it is. It's funny though, no matter how bad your life is sometimes, you still wouldn't swap it for anyone else's. You might say you would, but you wouldn't.

Trouble is, there's two more holidays to go before Steve finishes Year 12. And even then he might live at home. I don't know what he's applying for, and I don't think he'll get much anyway. He hasn't done any work since Easter, as far as I can tell.

Well, normal life resumes Monday, for better and for worse. At least it means you shouldn't have pages of Steve any more. So, good luck for Term 2 — lots of love,

Mandy

≈

May 8

Dear Mandy,

Well, like you I'm back at school. You sort of dread it in a way, but in another way it's not so bad, having something to do again. Not that I've been bored, but it's good seeing everyone.

Greg keeps ringing up, but he can't come down this way for a while, so everything's cool with

Casey. He doesn't know about Greg, and I plan to keep it that way.

As for your brother, I don't know. He sounds like a jerk. Don't you have a counsellor or something at your school? Those people who are meant to help when you've got a problem? I don't know how good they are but.

I'd get a knife and wait till he's asleep, then cut his balls off, tie a string round them and give them back to him for a yo-yo.

No, I didn't think of that myself. Wish I had. A girl here said it.

I'm watching TV while I'm doing this, but not concentrating. It's only the news. But listen to this: some English politician was on, and they were asking him about a car crash he was in. See, he survived this crash, but his chauffeur got killed. And he was smiling and laughing, and saying: 'Yeah, I guess someone up there likes me.' Now, you reckon you believe in God, so what I want to know is, did someone up there hate his chauffeur? I'm never going to cross the road again, if that's the way it works.

Hey listen Mandy, do you ever show these letters to anyone? Like Cheryl and them? I'm curious.

I don't show your letters to anyone.

Well, have a good term. Don't forget what I said about Steve. If that doesn't work, try microwaving his condoms (they shrink).

Love,
Tracey

≈

41

Dear Trace,

Thanks for your letter. I liked the bit about the car crash. The answer's simple: the guy on TV, the politician, is a nerd. I don't think God works that way. I think he creates it all, but after that he just lets it happen. But he gives you things like reflexes and brains, and your conscience, so that the world doesn't go crazy, and end in anarchy. And I think things like car crashes and people dying young of cancer and all that stuff are pure chance: out of a hundred people, one might die young, in a car accident or something, and it's pure luck (bad luck) if it happens to be you, or a friend of yours.

I've been lucky — the only people who've died in my family are one grandfather and one grandmother. My grandfather died when I was too young to remember, but my Nanna died two years ago, and that was awful. I still miss her, and I talk to her quite often — I have little chats to her inside my head and tell her what's happening and how I feel about things. She got burnt in the shower, but the worst thing was, my Poppa was at bowls and didn't get back till late, so she was there all day before they found her. She died the next day, in hospital.

We still go and put flowers on her grave. I'd like to go again soon — we haven't been in a while.

So I've got one of each left. Grandma (Dad's mum) lives in Speakman Bay, which means we don't see her often, and Poppa's in a home near here, and we go over about once a fortnight and take him food and stuff. He's so sweet but the home's depressing, even though it's a good one. I guess even the good ones are depressing. School's been OK so far. Today was above-average. There's this weird guy in our class, called Darren Small, and he does disgusting things like sticking pins through his skin and turning his eyelids inside out. He can fart 'Baa, Baa Black Sheep', he gives concerts when the teachers are late for class. He can do anything with his body. He is quite funny. Anyway he's got this big mouth — I mean literally — and he puts things in and takes them out again — like tennis balls, Poppers, stuff like that. He can fit his whole fist in his mouth.

So today, Paul Bazzani gave him this huge apple, the biggest I've ever seen, and told him to put that in. And Darren, being a bit of a Richard, did. There was only one problem: he couldn't get it out again. God, it was funny. We thought he might suffocate, he was going so red in the face, but I guess he could get air through his nose. Then Mr Prideaux arrived, for Geography, and after he grasped the situation (that took about ten minutes, which is fast for him), he went and got a knife and he had to cut bits out of the apple till Darren could get the rest out himself. Fair dinks, I nearly wet myself. Darren sure is one of life's losers. But it was funny.

Anyway, gotta go. Homework calls — not very loudly, but it does call. Oh by the way, thanks for the advice about the yo-yo and the condoms

43

— they're the only laughs I got out of the whole holidays. Is there a Plan C though? I don't think I've got the guts to try Plans A or B... though it's tempting.

See you,
        Love,
            Mandy

≈

Dear Mandy,

Thanks for your letter. Sorry if mine are getting boring. But don't stop writing, please. I love your letters. And I admire the way you write. Bet you get good marks in English. You seem so honest. I don't know how you do that.

Your writing about your grandparents made me think a lot, and remember a lot of things. I had this kind of flashback. I think I must have been staying at my Nanna's. And she gave me Coco Pops for breakfast, which would have been a big treat for me. Then she must have left the room, because I remember reaching over to get the milk and knocking my whole bowl on the floor. So what I did was to get down on the floor with the milk and my spoon, pour milk over the Coco Pops, and start eating. It must have seemed easier than picking up each Coco Pop. I can't remember what happened after that.

I would have been about three or four I suppose. We've got this English essay we're meant to be writing: 'Keep on Goin' till it all stops Flowin''. It seemed like a dumb topic at first, then I thought maybe I could write about Nanna. But I dunno. Among the people I don't trust are teachers and I don't like to write personal stuff that they can read and show other people. I poured my heart out in Year 7 once, in this journal we had to keep, and the teacher wrote at the bottom: 'Very good Tracey, keep writing.' Then they wonder why you don't bother.

School's a kind of drag already. What are you guys doing? I'll tell you our exciting topics. In Maths, quadratic functions; in English *To Kill a Mockingbird*; in History, the Industrial Revolution; in Geography, rainforests; in Chemistry, molecular structures...

Exciting isn't it?

What's your ambition in life? I heard a song the other day: 'Live fast, die young and leave a beautiful memory'. Or something like that. That's the way, isn't it?

See ya!

With love and depression,
Tracey

≈

Dear Trace

Thanks for your letter. I do like getting them. You know, when we started this I never thought it would last as long as it has. I was reading in the paper about these two old grannies who just got in *The Guinness Book of Records*. They've been writing to each other for seventy-eight years. I know you want to live fast and die young, but if you change your mind, let's go for the record, OK?

One of the old ladies is in Australia and the other is in England. They've met three times — once in Australia and twice in England. Wonder if, or when, we'll meet. I often think about it. It'd be strange. The worst thing would be if it was a real flop — like, if we didn't know what to say to each other. I'd hate that. But I don't think that would happen.

Which reminds me, you never sent a photo. OK, I know I didn't send you one either, but I was waiting for you to make the first move. You send me one and I'll send you one, fair enough?

If you saw me now you'd think I was the Freak Queen herself. I'm sitting here wearing Ug boots, track suit (we had netball this afternoon), two jumpers and a black Russian hat. It's so cold! I hate the cold weather. There's been thunder all day — just hanging around growling and scaring the dog. Then as I sat down to write this, a massive storm broke, and bombarded the house. It's still raining now — the roof's leaking over Steve's desk, so he's working in Katrina's room. Not that he does any work.

You asked me before if I show your letters to anyone, and I forgot to say. Yeah, I do show them to Cheryl sometimes. She's cool. She's just interested in how it all started. And I trust her totally. But if you don't want me to, I won't.

She was going to write to you too, but she never does half the things she says she will.

She came over here after netball for a while, with Rebecca. Bloody Rebecca's being a bitch again. She found out I like this guy in Year 11, George Vlahovic, and she went and told him! Fair dinkum, you'd trust her like you'd trust Jack the Ripper with a chain saw. George is cool about it but it's embarrassing. We're going out tomorrow night to a movie or something, but no thanks to Becca.

So, my love life's looking good for once. But that's about the only thing that is. We're doing *Mockingbird*, same as you, and we've got this massive assignment on it, due Monday, would you believe? He only gave us a week, and it's ten questions, 100 words on each. 'Mini essays' they have to be. So there goes the weekend.

Well, catch you round, like Rebecca's stomach. See you.

Love,
Mandy

≈

Dear Mandy,

So your love life's hotting up huh? You're a sly operator. Who is this guy? What happened to honest letters? Hope you had a good time Saturday night! Casey and I went out Saturday too. It was our first anniversary. We went to this really dressy restaurant, then to Blue Velvet. We didn't quit till 3 a.m. I was just warming-up but Case was starting to drag his feet.

Oh, I'm sick of writing this garbage, but I don't know what else to write about.

Tammy Wynette was just on TV, and they asked her why country music was so lasting. She said it was because it was simple and it was honest. I thought that was a good answer. Do you like country music? I don't mind it at all.

You remember that English essay I was telling you about? 'Keep on Goin' till it all stops Flowin''? Well, I wrote it like I said I would, about my Nanna, 'cos that's what her life was like — she kept fighting away, twenty-four hours a day, never giving up, till she broke her hip. It wrecked me when she died — I miss her so much. I swear to God, if that essay comes back with some dumb mark or comment on it, I'll turn it into confetti.

I honestly think it's the best essay I've ever written.

You know what my horoscope says today: 'Your past will cause you new complications but the solutions are in your hands. Expect good news about money, bad news about romance. Take special care when travelling but this is a good time to revisit old friends.'

The money part sounds OK.

Hey listen, what do your parents do? I mean, what jobs? You never said.

Bye. Write soon.

Lots of love,
Trace

≈

May 29

Trace, what's going on? The Greek exchange students had another meeting yesterday, and it was at Prescott High. Remember Prescott High? That's the school you said you go to. I had a letter for you, so I gave it to Phil — I thought a hand delivery'd be nicer, and faster.

Well, Phil checked at the office — they said they'd never heard of you. So he asked a few Year 10s — they'd never heard of you either. So he brought the letter back. Then I thought, maybe Phil's English isn't good enough and they didn't understand him. So I rang the office this morning — and guess what? I got the same answer as Phil.

So what is this? I can't believe you've changed schools and not told me. I found your old letter and it's there in black and white: Prescott High. I don't understand. Please write back.

Mandy

≈

Dear Mandy,

Don't worry about it — it's simple. The truth is,
I use a different name at school. Different surname,
that is. See, my father's not my father, he's my
stepfather. My real father died after I was born.
I reckon he took one look at me and carked it.
But I use his name for most things, like writing
to you. I only use my stepfather's name at school,
and that's because my brother and sister changed
to his. It causes some complications, but not often.

Sorry I didn't tell you before. I didn't think
it was important. And it never occurred to me that
you'd send a letter to the school.

So, hope that clears it up. Do I get my letter
now?

Lots of love,
Trace

≈

Trace, I'm no Sherlock Holmes, but this is still
bugging me. You said, a long time back, that your
parents have been married for twenty-five years.
Now you say your father died after you were born.

Something sucks. Please write back.

Mandy

≈

June 13

Dear Tracey,

It's been a long while since your last letter, the longest gap ever. What's going down? I don't understand what you've been doing. Please write back and level with me — I need to know.

Love,
Mandy

≈

June 20

Trace, don't do this to me. I can hack anything except silence. If you want to stop writing, that's OK, I guess, although I don't want to stop. But I've got to know the truth, at least. Please answer this letter.

Love,
Mandy

≈

June 26

Dear Trace,

I'm going to write every day if I have to, until I get an answer. To tell you the truth, I'm a bit scared about this now. Cheryl said something that freaked me out. I mean, in one way, I don't know

51

much about you. I don't know where you live, or what school you go to. I don't have a photo of you. I'm not even sure if I know your name any more. Like Cheryl said, maybe you're a psycho or something. But you know, I don't think you are. I've got to trust myself, and my feelings, and I really believe that you're an OK person. But I think you've been bullshitting me a lot. When I go back over your letters, there's some funny things. For example, you seem to have lost a dog and gained a horse somewhere. I think I can almost tell which bits are real and which bits are fake. So I hope you write at least once more and tell me what the hell's going on.

Love (I think),
Mandy

≈

POSTCARD   June 29

I'm not giving up. One week of term left — I'll haunt you these holidays. Just tell me the truth, please.   *M.*

≈

July 3

Stop hassling me. Leave me alone. Can't you take a hint? And don't send any more postcards. People here read them.

≈

Tracey, what do you mean 'people here read them'? Where are you for Christ's sake? For that matter, who are you?

School finished today, but I'll be here all holidays. Just me and Stevie Wonder. I've got enough to be scared about, without you sending weird messages. That 'people here read them' freaked me right out.

Are you in trouble? If we're friends, then we can tell each other anything, can't we?

Anyway, I need to keep writing to you. Our letters have been good for me. They help keep me going.

Please write.

Love, *Mandy*

≈

July 13

Dear Trace,

It's a week since my last letter and still no answer. At first I thought I'd start sending you postcards with strange messages, to force you to write. But I read all your letters again today, and I've decided that I've got to keep trusting you, no matter what.

I've got to trust someone. George Vlahovic dumped me at the beginning of the holidays, after an interesting few weeks; Cheryl's gone to Red Point with her family for a fortnight; Rebecca keeps secrets like Henry VIII kept wives (see, I've learnt some History this year); Katrina's never home, Maria's working in her parents' shop ... it doesn't leave much. I've tried to talk to Mum and Dad again, not just about Steve, about everything. Well it was Mum I tried to talk to mainly. And she tried, she really did, but she was tired and the things she said weren't much help. I told her about George for example, and she was saying, 'Well you're too young for a serious relationship,' and 'I know it seems like the end of the world at your age, but you do get over it.'

Hell, maybe she's right.

You know even writing that paragraph has made me feel better! I'd like to get this going again.

Love,
Mandy

≈

July 18

Mandy, I'm sorry I've let you down but there's nothing I can do about it. You wouldn't understand — and you wouldn't want to know, believe me. Let's forget the whole thing, OK?

Tracey

≈

July 20

Come on Trace, give me a bit of credit. You know, looking back, I trusted you from the start and I don't think you ever trusted me at all. Try me now — you might be surprised. *M*.

≈

July 30

Dear Trace,

Well no-one can say I don't try. I've thought of five thousand reasons why all this might have happened but I don't have a clue.

Third term's started. There's so much work. Trouble is, all the students want to be slack, because they know they've got to work hard next year, but all the teachers want us to start now.

What school do you go to? You could be at Prescott High under another name I suppose, but somehow I don't think so.

What mark did you get for the essay about your grandmother? That part was real, wasn't it? I can tell. Hope you got a big juicy A.

In your last real letter you asked what my parents do. Well, my mother's a reference librarian at the State Library and my father's a wardsman at St Francis' Hospital, which is only about one k away from here.

And you asked whether I like country music. Well I don't much, although a couple of them are OK.

Hope you're OK but I'm not too sure that you are. Something tells me you're in bad shape. I care a lot about what happens to you. So, take care.

Love,
Mandy

≈

August 1

Mandy,

OK wise guy, you asked for it, you want to keep snooping around my life I'll tell you the truth but you're not going to like it. You heard of Garrett? Well if you haven't I'll tell you. It's a maximum security place, where they put you if you're bad, and if you're worse than bad they put you in A Block, and that's where I am and that's where I've been for eleven months and that's where they're going to try to keep me for a long time yet, but not if I have any say they won't. So now fuck off and get out of my life.

≈

Aug 10

Well, that sure worked didn't it? Thought it would. Now you know why I never told you in the first place. So thanks for proving me right.

≈

Tracey, that's not fair. I've started about ten letters since you finally wrote, but I couldn't finish any. None of them seemed right. I don't know if this'll finish in the rubbish tin like the others. I don't have a clue what to say. Your letter blew me away. I admit that. But at least now I can guess why you put the ad in, and I can see why you didn't tell the truth about where you were.

I looked up Garrett in a telephone directory and a street directory and I've been trying to find out a bit about it. But it's not easy.

I honestly don't know what to write. I think all I can do is send this off and hope you'll answer. And I really hope you do.

See you,
Mandy

≈

I don't know what to write either. I only put the ad in as a joke, one day when I was sitting round with nothing to do (like every day). I never meant it to end up like this.

Keep writing if you want. But don't expect much back. I wouldn't know what to say.

Tracey

≈

Dear Tracey,

Thanks for writing back. I'm still in a state of shock, I admit, but something makes me keep writing. I'm curious about you of course — don't be offended — it's just that I thought I was getting to know you and now I find I don't know you at all. And I do feel ripped-off, because there I was pouring my heart out to you, and now I wonder if you've been laughing at me and showing my letters to your mates so they could all share the joke.

I don't think you would, mind you, because I still think I know you a bit, but it's a matter of trust I guess.

So what's the true story?

I thought I'd bring you up to date with what's happening in my life, but it's harder now. It seems so insignificant compared to the kind of life you must have. And it's so long since I wrote you a 'proper' letter, I can't remember what I told you. I think I was still with George then. That does seem a long time ago. Anyway, he dropped me a while back, no special reason, we're still good mates, blah blah blah.

So, what can I write that's going to interest you? I don't know any more. I've got the same problem as you — I don't know what to say either.

I hope you write again but.

Mandy

≈

Dear Mandy,

Don't you understand? The reason I put the ad in? I wanted to know what a real life was like. I wanted to know what normal people do. That's why I liked your letters. That's what I want you to write about. I wanted you to write about your family and school and all that shit. I wanted you to be normal, the world's most normal person. That's why I hated hearing about your brother, because when you started talking about him, and the fights and everything, you were sounding like me or anyone else here. And I didn't want that. Twenty-four hours a day is enough.

So that's all you have to write about. It's easy for you.

And I don't show your letters to anyone, although I don't blame you for wondering. And I don't laugh at them. In my twelve months (nearly) yours (and the other ones from the ad) are the only letters I've had.

You asked a while back about my Nanna essay. Well, seeing you asked, I'll tell you: it got an A+ and the teacher said she was going to enter it in a competition. See, I can do some things. And not everything I told you was bullshit.

Have you told Cheryl and them about me? About being in Garrett I mean?

Tracey

Dear Tracey,

Sheez, instead of not knowing what to say, this time I don't know where to start.

Congratulations about your essay. That's great. I'm not surprised though, 'cos you do write well. Am I allowed to see it?

But why do you keep saying you don't know what to write about? Write about yourself. Write about Garrett. You think I'm not burning up to know more about you? Just what is true in what you told me before? Like I said, I think I can tell what's fake and what isn't, but in some parts it's not easy. What's true about your family for instance?

As for my telling people, well, I told Cheryl that you didn't go to Prescott High, and I couldn't get you to answer my letters. That's when she said you might be some psycho. But I haven't told her you're in Garrett. I was too freaked-out by it all. She keeps asking me, but I tell her I haven't heard. I'll have to say something eventually but at the moment I don't seem to want to, I don't know why.

I haven't told anyone else. I'm still hanging around with Cheryl, but not so much with Rebecca or Maria. I'm good mates with a girl called Naomi Barker, plus a new girl called Mai Huynh, from Vietnam. As you may have guessed, this is a bit of a multi-cultural school — 28 different languages or something, including heaps of Vietnamese, but

Mai's the only Vietnamese I've got to know well. She's sweet, but she can be a bit of a suck.

I suppose my family is sort of normal. I'd never thought of us that way. Except for Steve, but every family has to have one creep. There's no zoo without a gorilla.

Am I allowed to ask what you did to get put in Garrett?

You know, a lot of things are making sense to me now. Why you wouldn't send me a photo — guess you don't have any. Why you didn't ring me up, or send me your phone number. Are you allowed phone calls? Why you have a post-office box. Maybe even why you don't believe in God.

How come they don't censor your letters?

I can't believe the way my innocent letter to you, back in February I think it was, has developed into this. Oh well, maybe it was meant to be. Anyway, it'd be good to get a long letter back this time.

Love,
Mandy

≈

Sep 4

Dear Mandy,

The one thing I did think when I got sent here was that I wouldn't have to do schoolwork. And it's true you don't have to go to the classes. But there's nothing else to do, so you go. And when you do, you get more work than at real school. (Not Prescott High, either. Jefferis High was the last, but there've been a few.) I don't normally give a, so I don't do much, but lately I've been trying a bit, for some stupid reason, and it's too hard. I mean tonight I spent an hour and a half on one problem in Maths and got nowhere. Trouble is, there's no-one to ask. And then tomorrow the stupid bat'll tell me I should make an effort. 'You've got brains, Tracey you should use them.'

Well, suppose I better answer the questions in your letter. But the lights go out in half an hour, so don't expect any ten-pager.

You're right about the photos — I don't have any of me. This place is pretty strict. You know how you see on TV all these modern Qs with carpets and colour TV and pinnies? There may be some like that somewhere, but I've never seen one. Maybe I'm in the wrong state — this girl from Jennings reckons they're OK there. When you get here you're given a list of the rules, and what you can keep in your slot. Here it is, if you're interested:

H.M. DETENTION CENTRE
GARRETT

NOTICE

Do not deface your cell or other Garrett property.
No gambling will be permitted.
You have been received into this centre either on
    remand or to serve a term of imprisonment.
If you consider you have grounds for appeal you
    may ask to see a legal adviser.

62

The following kit and equipment will be permitted in cells.

1 bed (fixed)	1 pkt tampons or
1 mattress cover	sanitary napkins
blankets as issued	6 photographs (not
1 pillow	mounted)
1 pillow slip	1 towel
2 sheets	1 unbacked mirror
1 plastic mug	1 toilet roll
1 ashtray	1 biro type pen
1 picture H.M. Queen	6 letters
1 desk (fixed)	2 newspapers as
1 seat (fixed)	authorized
1 cupboard (fixed)	3 library books
1 tablet of soap	2 magazines
1 toothbrush	1 tablet of writing
1 tube toothpaste	paper

Articles and books required for educational purposes:
A cell card listing such articles, and initialled by the Education Officer, must be kept in your cell. An exception is made for items issued by class-room tutors and containing an authorisation slip.

F.R. Batchelor
(Director of Prisons)

Pretty exciting, hey?

But they let you have some stuff that's not on the list. Time's running out. But before the lights go off, I want to say one thing: Don't ask why I got put in here. Don't try to find out. If you do, that'll be the end of any friendship, for a good reason — you won't want to have anything to do with me.

You see? It's never going to be much of a friendship, is it? Because I can't be honest. If I don't pretend and act and cover up you'll realize how off I am. So either we have a friendship that's half-fake, or I'm honest and we lose it. All that crap you see on posters, like 'True friends are truthful friends', it doesn't work when you give it the acid test.

Lights out — see ya
Tracey

September 10

Dear Trace,

Why do your letters take so long to get to me? Last time I asked, you gave me some fake excuse. Is it because they do censor them?

I'm still spinning round and out. God, Trace, I don't know what you did. I can't imagine. It scares me, to tell you the truth. But I've got to stick tight to a few things — one of them being that I think you're OK. All these months of letters, I know a lot of what you said wasn't true, but you can't hide yourself completely, and I think, reading between the lines, that you're an OK person.

Maybe you did do something really bad. I guess you must have. But I bet you wouldn't do anything like that now. And there are all kinds of reasons why people do stuff. Maybe you were hanging round with the 'wrong crowd', as my mother calls them. (She means anyone with a tat or rad hair). The good old peer group pressure that we get warned about at assembly every second day. Maybe you were off your face, or worse. Doing drugs. I don't know. This is foreign country to me.

The counsellor at school told Steve he'd end up in Ruxton if he didn't watch out.

Sheez, this term's been a long one. I suppose winter term always is. Netball's been good — we won a few games. Finished second last, but still. It seemed like every weekend was raining — wet and cold and windy. I've been trying to teach Mai Huynh to play netball but fair dinkum, you've never seen anything like it. She'd rather let the ball bounce off her head than catch it. I don't think girls play much sport in Vietnam. But she's teaching me table tennis and she's a star at that. So don't ask me to explain it.

That was true about your basketball team, wasn't it? All that stuff you wrote?

Went to the movies with Naomi (Barker) and Cheryl yesterday. Nay and I both wanted to see *Waiting for You*, but Cheryl talked us into going to *David's Diary*. She sure likes to get her own way. But *David's Diary* was good. It's about this guy who's rapt in this girl named Alex, and she's got an identical twin named Sarah. And the two girls keep swapping on him, 'cos Alex doesn't like him much anyway. And after a while Sarah decides she's got the hots for him. Then Alex decides there must be more to him than she realized, so she gets interested too. But now he's switched to Sarah... and so it goes on. It's sort of a comedy, but a romance too.

Do you get videos where you are? How much TV can you watch?

Well, hear from you soon I hope.

Love,
Mandy

≈

Sep 12

Dear Mandy,

OK, big-nose, you want answers, let's get them out of the way. I swear, you ought to be a welfare officer.

1. They say they do 'random censoring' (spot checks) of letters in and out. We have to hand them in unsealed, and the ones we get have been opened. But the hacks (they're the guards), the ones we talk to, say they don't bother much, except to look for drugs. Round about Christmas they started reading everything, and there was a full-on riot. So they're a bit nervous of doing it now.

2. Of course all the basketball stuff was true. That's our big thrill here — if you suck up enough

bums you get to play sport once a week (it's really more like once a fortnight — if you're lucky) with outside teams. No away games unfortunately, or they'd come back with an empty bus. There's a gym here and teams from outside come in to play. They're only adults — no kids our age allowed. Most of them are hacks and their friends and rellies, or Christians, people like that. But basketball's the best, because that's the only sport where we're in a regular comp., with finals and everything. And they always play the finals in here, whether we're in them or not, 'cos they say we've got the best gym. But maybe it's 'cos they're sorry for us.

Trouble is, we might get kicked out of the comp. soon — they reckon we play too rough. But if they want to see rough they ought to come into the yard for five minutes. That's rough. They expect us to be real thugs, so the moment we brush them with a fingernail they drop to the ground and cry. I gotta go to the next question. This is getting me mad, thinking about it.

3. I haven't got that essay about my Nanna at the moment. The teacher's still got it. But when I get it back — oh I don't know. I'd be embarrassed to have you read it.

4. I guess the reason my letters take so long is that they're slack here about sending them. We take them to breakfast and put them in a box. I don't know what happens to them then.

5. One of the slags (that's us) told me the reason they use a post-office box is so people won't get embarrassed. Like, if your grey-haired grannie goes

into her country post office with a letter addressed to her dear granddaughter in Garrett, or if she gets a letter with Garrett written on the back of the envelope, then everyone'll know. So it all goes through a box number.

6. We can watch TV for an hour in the afternoon, after school lessons; an hour after tea; and an hour during the day at weekends. But it's only black and white. No video, although they keep promising. (It doesn't take long in here to get jacked-off with promises.) And there are the worst fights over what to watch. Some shows everyone agrees on, but not many. Half the time the hack tells you what it's going to be, just to stop the fights.

Well, this is about my longest letter ever. Oh yeah, one last thing: tell your brother to stay out of Ruxton if he knows what's good for him. That's Vaseline City in there, believe me. KY Country. On the other hand, maybe you'd think he deserved it.

OK, gotta go. See you.

Tracey

≈

September 17

Dear Trace,

Thanks for the letter. It was good. You know, last night I was down the park with Anonymous Dog, chasing him around and throwing sticks and being stupid, and in the middle of it all I tried to imagine

68

what you'd be doing at that exact time (it was 5.25) and what that place would look like and everything. I don't know why — I suppose it was the contrast between the park and Garrett. It was hard to imagine but.

It's funny, before, I used to envy you so much. You sounded like you had it all — money, pets, a horse, great holidays, wonderful boyfriends, a family who cared. Guess it was too good to be true. Maybe no-one has it all. None of it was true, was it? Reading back, it's like those parts of your letters seem dead. Is the reason you wrote all that because that's the way you'd like it to be? What's the truth about your family? The exact opposite? When you said you never got any letters, I wondered. Are you allowed to have visitors? Do you get any? Apart from basketballers that is.

Now when I write about the problems of my life, they seem trivial. Although Steve's the only big one, and I guess he's not trivial.

I was talking to Mum in the kitchen last night. She was having a coffee and doing the crossword — those cryptic ones, that make no sense to me. I was asking her about friends and all that. I asked her whether her friends had ever given her the palm at school, whether there'd been much back-stabbing. See, Rebecca's really dark with me lately. And Mum was saying how it wasn't that complicated when she was at school. She said everyone was friendly and because it was a small school and in the country, everyone had to get on or there'd be no-one to talk to. She said life was simple —

they'd go for a swim or sit round in the milk bar after school. Going to the movies was a real rage. And she was saying how it didn't seem like a simple life to them then, but when she compares it to the way things are now, she realizes it was.

Maybe when we're 45 we'll look back on these times and think it was all simple. Doubt it but. Drugs, violence, porn, AIDS, ozone layers — I can't handle it. You know what Paul Bazzani asked in Science today: 'Sir, can you get AIDS from killing a mozzie and eating it?' Fair dinkum, he's such a drop-kick. But you gotta laugh.

Hey, speaking of porn, there's a movie tonight called *Reform School Girls*, at about midnight. Have you ever seen it? It sounds like a bit of a porn effort. Can't imagine it's much like real life in Garrett. Which reminds me: when do you get out of there? And my last question for this letter — when's your birthday? Hope I haven't missed it.

Time I went to bed. Bye for now. Take care, Trace — heaps of it.

Love,
Mandy

PS: Do you follow the same terms as us? We finish Friday. But we're not going anywhere.

≈

Dear Mandy,

Two days of school to go — yes, we do have the
same holidays as you guys. I'm spending these
holidays in Bali with my kind, rich parents and
my nice brother and sister. Oh yeah, and my lover
Casey — the one who looks like Jim Morrison.
But don't worry, I'll bring you back some pressies
— a colour TV, a CD player, French perfume,
clothes — just a few bits and pieces paid for out
of my pocket money...

You know what I'd like right now? A Supreme
Pizza, family size, with chewy cheese, and heaps
of salami and tomato and anchovies and mush-
rooms. And covered with olives. Have you seen
that ad on TV where the guys are marooned in
a lifeboat, and they take it in turns to describe
the meal they'd like if they could choose? We go
crazy when that comes on. Everyone yells and
chucks stuff at the TV.

You get obsessed with food here. It becomes
the most important thing in your life. Oh, I dunno,
I guess sex rates high too. But food! I'd give a
year of my life for a pizza or a quarter-pounder
or a box of Darrell Leas. The thing is, you get
plenty of food here, but it's muck. Tonight was
typical: sausages and three vegetables. But the sausages were those big greasy ones and the vegetables
were mushy and watery. There's always bread, and
jam if you're fast enough, and milk, so you pig
out on those. And then you get fat and your skin

gets worse and worse. There are people in here with faces where you could play join the dots.

Suppose I'd better keep answering your questions. You ask more bloody questions than a shrink. My birthday was 6 July. I was 16. You missed it but don't worry, I got heaps of presents — a new horse, pair of skis, my own keycard, no limit. My father's giving me a BMW when I turn 18...

Now do you see how I keep from going mad in here?

Ah, I hate it, I hate it, I fucking hate it. I can't write anymore.

≈

September 24

Dear Trace,

Your letter came today — third day of the holidays. You sounded pretty desperate. I hope you're OK. Keep writing, whatever you do. God, I wish I could help in some way — I feel so helpless. Acacia Park seems a long way from Garrett. And I don't mean in kilometres, although it's that too.

I don't know what you did to get put in there but I can't believe it was anything that bad. I think you just must have got a few bad breaks. I can't believe you're a bad person — I feel I know you too well by now.

Well, what next? You said you wanted me to write about my 'normal' life, so guess I better do that. But if you want it, you've got to take it all. I'm not going to leave out the dark side or the bad times just because you want to believe real life's happy and peaceful. It ain't. Here in the suburbs... there's plenty of ugly moments. Anyway, you must know that. Where did you live before you got sent to Garrett?

Still, things are good at the moment. Dad got me a couple of days' work at the hospital, starting tomorrow, to replace someone who's hurt her ankle. I was meant to be doing work experience these holidays anyway, and I hadn't organized anything, so this is a good way out. And money! Beautiful money! Hope the lady breaks her other ankle and takes a few weeks off. No, not really. But I'm looking forward to it.

Cheryl's coming round in a minute, so this'll be a short letter, by my standards. We're going to a friend's place. I'm doing a bit of a number with this guy called Adam Tisdall, in Year 12. And I've got the love bites to prove it. Someone told me to put toothpaste on them, but I don't know which is worse — walking round with love bites on your neck, or walking round with big gobs of toothpaste. Anyway, Cheryl's with a mate of Adam's, called Justin Smith, who did Year 12 last year — now he's doing a sheet metal apprenticeship. They're both good guys — they're so funny — you're wetting yourself when you're with them. Only because they're funny, mind you.

Just realized what the time was. I have to go. It seems unfair that I'm off to have a good time when you can't — and like I said, I wish I could say or do something that'd pick you up while you're feeling bad. Hope by the time you get this things have improved. But I know time doesn't fix everything — and neither do words.

See you —
Love,
Mandy

≈

Sep 26

Dear Mandy,

I don't think there's any point in keeping this going. It's so fake. You think I'm a nice person who's had a few bad breaks, huh? Well, OK, keep thinking that if you want, it's no skin off my nose. You talk about the dark side of your life — you don't know what dark is. This is a hole and I'm the biggest bitch in it. If you only knew. You're the one person I'm — I don't know what the word is — soft with. That's because you're not in here. If you were in here, you'd see me like I am, and if you didn't see me you'd hear about me.

I'm not whingeing. I deserved what I got, maybe more. But I'm sick of pretending to you. And I'm scared I'm getting softer, the more I write to you. I can't afford that. I'm buried in here and the only thing that matters to me is being King Dick. Which I am. And loving it. So, screw you.

T.

≈

Tracey, don't write that kind of crap to me. I'm not taking it from you. The truth is, you haven't been faking at all. You've just been letting your good side come out. And you're scared that people will think you're weak, because of it. Well I've got news for you. You can't get rid of it, because it's there, it's part of you, and it's going to keep coming out, no matter how much you try to stop it. Just like a zit. So stop fighting it. And I've got another piece of news for you. I'm going to keep writing to you, no matter what. Even if you don't answer. I'll just keep writing, like I did before. Because you invited me into your life, and you're stuck with me, whether you like it or not. So screw you.

Now I'm going to write about my life and my 'normal' boring old family and friends, and you can sit there and read it. And don't you dare put this letter down. OK. Where do I start? Item 1: I worked three days at the hospital, made $261, $208 after deductions, but I'll get a lot of that back. I had a great time but I sure was tired. I did all kinds of jobs, from mopping up blood and vomit, to feeding little old men with no teeth. But it was cool fun. One old guy, must have been about ninety, kept trying to crack onto me, wanting my phone number and everything. And I met Paul Strazzera, who was in there for a knee reconstruction and I got his autograph. He was so nice! And I learnt how to operate a switchboard (I made friends with a girl working there). I had a rad time!

Item 2: Adam Tisdall continues to be item no. 1 with me. I saw him every day when I was working at the hospital, and I'm seeing him again tomorrow, and we're going to some nightclub next weekend (my parents don't know yet, but).

Item 3: The dog just broke one of Mum's favourite plates — he jumped against the table, trying to catch a fly, so his life expectancy's now been cut by fifty per cent.

Item 4: Steve was actually nice to me today — he bought me Aphrodite's first album, *Anodyne Necklace*, because he saw it on special at Tozers', and he knew I wanted it. I just about passed out.

So that's the state of my life right now. What you read is what you get. Kindly write back.

Yours faithfully (you better believe it),
Mandy

≈

Oct 3

Mandy, something fantastic's happened. It's so good I'm pinching myself. I can't even write it down in case it goes away. I'll write to you tomorrow.

Love,
Tracey

PS: Thanks for the letter.

≈

Dear Mandy,

Well, you better keep all our letters kiddo, and get ready to sell them for a fortune in a few years 'cos I'm gonna be famous! (And not like I was before, either.) You remember that essay? 'Keep on Goin' till it all stops Flowin'?' Well, our English tutor, Mrs McKinnon, put it in a competition, like she said she would. And it won! She told me Wednesday, but I wouldn't believe it till the letter came today. You get $500 (not that that's much good to me in here), and a set of books (not much good either) and the best of all, the story gets published in a book that's coming out next year. Can you believe it? I can't. And what I like is they don't know I'm in Garrett — Mrs McKinnon used the post-office box — so it's no charity deal. They would have thought I was just anyone.

So, guess I'd better let you read it now, after all that. Here goes:

KEEP ON GOIN' TILL IT ALL STOPS FLOWIN'
'Where are we today, Nanna?' I asked.
She looked at me with her tired, confused eyes.
'Don't be silly Jan,' she said, 'And don't you go running off. I've got a lot of shopping to do, and I want to catch the four o'clock bus. You can help carry the bags.'
The only trouble was, we weren't at the shops and my name isn't Jan. Jan was my aunt, and she died years ago.
I visited Nanna every day and sat by her bed for

hours, talking to her. I don't think she understood much of it. One minute, according to her, we were watching TV at home; the next minute she'd be getting me ready for school (only she thought I was my mother); then a bit later we'd be at next door's having coffee.

Nanna wasn't really in any of these places. She was in hospital. She'd been knocked over by a kid on a bike and had broken her hip. She'd had an operation, but when she woke up it was like her mind had gone away. Every day was the same: she never seemed to improve.

One afternoon I was sitting there when the doctor came to look at her. He talked to me while he was doing it.

'She could go on like this for a long time,' he said. 'It's like everything's gone from her, but her body's still alive. Her heart's beating on. The machine's running but the factory's closed.'

I thought it was cruel of him to talk about Nanna like that in front of her, but I guess she didn't understand.

When Nanna stopped eating, I started making deals with God. 'If you get her to eat again, I'll give up smoking,' I said. The next day I checked with the nurse when I got there.

'Yes, she's been a good girl today' she said. 'She just had a sandwich and a cup of soup.'

So I quit smoking.

A few nights later I was riding home on the bus, after seeing Nanna. She'd been hopeless — talking to her own reflection in the mirror, raving about men trying to pick her up. I don't think she even knew I was in the room. It was depressing. So I made another deal. 'If you let her recognize me then I'll stop jigging school.'

That was Friday. On Sunday I'd been in there about half an hour when suddenly she opened her eyes and said, in her normal clear voice: 'Hello Tracey honey, how long have you been here?'

'Only a few minutes,' I said. 'You were asleep.'

We talked for about ten minutes before she dozed off. She knew where she was, she knew what had happened to her, she was asking about everyone and how they were going. The only time she got confused was when she thought Poppa was still alive.

Round about this time of my life I'd been getting involved with a guy called Blue, and his mates. They didn't have a very good reputation, and that's putting it mildly. They were a lot older than me and they all had bikes, big ones. They were a gang I guess. So there was a lot of pressure on me to keep away from them — I had counsellors, teachers, even friends, telling me not to get involved.

So I made my final deal with God.

'Make Nanna get better and I'll drop Blue.'

Nanna died five days later, while I was holding her hand. The same doctor was there when it happened. 'Everything stops eventually' he said. 'There's no need to cry.'

I wasn't crying. Blue and his mates were heading north next day. I went with them, riding on the back of Blue's BM. We had a lot of laughs.

Well, that's it. Pretty crappy hey?

See you
> Love,
>> *Trace*

PS: This is the only thing I've ever won. Funny I had to come in here to win something.

≈

October 8

Trace, what's happened? Don't do this to me! Write back IMMEDIATELY, OK? God, I hope it's something really good. Your note drove me crazy! There'd better be something in the mail tomorrow! Gotta rush. Love, *M.*

≈

October 10

Dear Trace,

AAAAAAAAAAAAAAAAAAAAGGGGGGHHHHH-HHHHHHHHHH! Could you hear me screaming, even from inside A Block? You must have! I was more excited than if I'd won it myself! But seriously, you must have known you'd win. The story was so fantastic, it couldn't have lost. It made me cry — you sure can write.

When does this book come out exactly? I can't wait. I'll buy heaps of copies and give them to everyone and say: 'I know this person! I know her! Someone famous!' Hope it's a paperback, so I can afford it.

How come the money's no good to you in Garrett? Aren't you allowed any money? God, they must be strict.

I'm not game to ask how much of the story's true. Well, I am game. How much of the story's true? But you don't have to answer if you don't want. Actually you're pretty good at not answering

80

things you don't want to — I've asked about your family before and so far you've managed to tell me exactly zero.

Wish I had anything exciting to tell you, but life's dull here. I sure haven't won anything. This is the third day back. Do you realize we'll be in Year 11 after this term? I feel like I've only just started high school. They say the jump from Year 10 to Year 11 is bigger than the jump from 11 to 12. Well, we'll soon find out.

I'm still with Adam but Cheryl's having a rocky time with Justin. Rebecca's got glandular, not badly, but she's not back yet. I'm going to Mai Huynh's tonight to help with her English. Pity you aren't here — you could take over the teaching. This'll be the first time I've met her parents — it'll be interesting.

Well, Trace, I gotta tell you, I'm fair dinkum rapt about your story. You could be bigger than Virginia Andrews. Actually you write a lot better than Virginia Andrews. So, keep on goin' till it all stops flowin', OK? Love you heaps,

Mandy

≈

Oct 12

Dear Mandy

Thanks a lot for your letter. You are good to tell things to. But winning this thing hasn't been that great. I didn't tell anyone here, but Mrs McKinnon

81

did. And somehow it gave some of the hacks and even some of the slags — that's us — the idea that I was going soft. OK, yeah, it's like you said in your letter. So they started brown-nosing round. And I had to put on an act to let them know I was as big a bitch as ever. So now I'm on PS — Punishment Sheets — and I nearly got worse.

PS (Pure Shit) means you scrub floors and clean toilets and stuff. It can be slack or bad, depending on who's on. Today was Mrs Neumann, and she's bad news. She hates my guts. So every job I did, it was like, 'Do it again.' No reasons, no explanation, just 'Do it again.' I'm stuffed tonight. And at the end she said, 'Now try writing a story about PS.' Really sarcastic.

A few months ago she came into the common room. It was Saturday afternoon and we were having our big thrill, our hour of TV. She said she had a phone message for me. We're not allowed to take calls, but people can leave messages if there's a special reason. I put out my hand for it without looking at her, and she cracked. Started screaming about how the trouble with me was that I didn't know my place, and how she was going to teach it to me. She was saying I thought I was King Dick and everything. She said if I wanted the message I had to kneel down. I sat there for about three minutes, then I did it. No-one'll ever know what it cost me to do that. But Mandy, I'd been in here six months, and no contact from anyone, except your letters. So I did it. Even though it was in front of the others, I still did it.

But that wasn't enough. She was loving it. No-one was watching TV any more — they were watching me. She said, 'Hands and knees Tracey.' Then she ripped off a few more comments about teaching me my place. I was still kneeling, and she said again, 'Get on your hands and knees if you want it.'

Well, I couldn't do it. I knelt there, only half listening, then I dived at her. But she was expecting that. She jumped back, some other hacks grabbed me, they chucked me back in my slot for the weekend, and that was the last I heard about my phone message.

Monday I even asked her politely for it, but she walked away. Trouble is, I don't know if there ever was a message. She could have been faking it, to set me up.

How'd I get onto all this? Oh yeah, explaining what a bitch Mrs Neumann is. So anyway, all I'm saying is that they haven't exactly been chucking parties here for me.

Mandy, can you do me a big favour? Please? This is the only thing I've asked you for (I think). Can you get a bottle of champagne and drink it for me, to celebrate? With some friends, if you want, but don't say what it's for. Then write and tell me about it. I really want you to do this.

With love,

Trace

≈

Dear Trace,

Thanks heaps for the card. I didn't think you'd remember. It was beautiful — you're really artistic. That's at least two things I know you're good at. Did you write the poem? It was so funny.

It was a good birthday for once. Had about twenty people round for a barbecue. Mum and Dad kept a low profile, Steve sulked in his room (his exams start soon), Katrina was home. So that was all good. We partied till about one o'clock. Adam came, and gave me a beautiful silver chain. He's getting serious. Mum and Dad gave me a bike — good one too, once I figure out how to use the gears. But it's got two wheels and a seat and a chain and handlebars and everything, so can't complain. No, seriously, it's what I asked for. I want to get fit. Steve gave me a helmet to go with the bike, but Mum and Dad would have paid for it, nothing surer. Katrina gave me two stunning shirts, both from Daniel. One's black with silver lining, sort of cowboy style, with a big silver star on the left boob, the other's thin red, white and blue stripes, two pockets, short sleeves, really smart. She's so nice — she's always broke herself and these must have cost a fortune. I'll have to get her something extra good for Christmas.

I got lots of little pressies from the people at the party and a book from Cheryl, called *Confederacy of Dunces*, which looks rad. Mai gave me a beautiful Vietnamese vase, so delicate, with tiny blue flowers on it. And Naomi Barker gave me a Power Without Glory CD that I didn't have. (*PWG* — their second one. It's the one with 'Dining at the Y' on it.)

Then Saturday night Adam and I went to a school dance. It was a sort of farewell for the Year 12s. Bit of a joke 'cos I went and Steve didn't. But what I had to tell you was, on the way there I made Adam pull in at a bottle shop and get a bottle of champagne. Then we went down the river, where there's lots of space. I'd brought two glasses from home and we sat there for about half an hour talking and drinking. He kept wanting to know what it was for but I wouldn't tell him. But I drank a toast to you, a silent toast.

So that was your celebration party. Not as good as you deserve but the best I could do. Hope you like it.

You know, that story about Mrs Neumann — I honestly don't think I'd survive life in there. I've been thinking about it a lot. I couldn't sleep, the night I read your letter. Why do people act like that? What makes them do such things? I don't understand the human race. My dog looks better all the time. I don't know how you face up to each day.

I know this is another delicate question, and you ignore the ones you don't want to answer anyway, but is there any chance you'll be out for Christmas? I thought people got so much time off for good behaviour these days that they never stayed in for long.

Well, thinking of you. Take care.

Love,
   Mandy

≈

Dear Mandy,

No, I won't be out for Christmas. To get time off for good behaviour, your behaviour has to be good. Anyway what do you think I'm in here for — nicking a Mars Bar? Riding the trains without a ticket? Overdue library books?

No offence Mandy, but you seem bloody innocent sometimes.

It's funny, I go to so much trouble not to whinge about this place when I'm writing to you. I don't want you to know how bad it is. And I go to so much trouble to be 'nice'. Don't want to scare you off. But I guess a bit leaks through.

Thanks for having my celebration for me. I knew I could rely on you. I'll pay you back one day.

I think maybe they're right about me and I am getting soft. There's this new girl in here, Anita Kelly, who's busting her gut (and she's got a big one) to be the biggest slag in the whole valley. And to do that, she's gotta get past me. And you know something? I might let her. I can't be bothered anymore, somehow. I look at her and think 'Go for it, Anita. You think you can stand the heat, I'll even lend you the matches.' Fair dinkum, she's the biggest slut you ever saw in your life. I reckon she's into the golden grommet, and don't ask what that means. She's in here for RWV — you might have seen it on the news. It was a bad one.

Well, while I'm in the mood to write about this place I guess I better answer some of these questions you've been firing at me again. But there are some things I can't talk about, OK? All that family stuff especially.

So, first question, when do I get out of here? That's easy. I get out of here when I'm 18. On my happy eighteenth birthday. Yep, I get out of here — straight across the road to Macquarie Women's Prison. I stay there till I'm 20 and four months, give or take a few years.

We're allowed visitors once a week, but in here (Maximum S I mean) they've got to be approved, and you have screens between you and all that junk. I don't have any visitors anyway.

And you asked where I used to live. Well, I've moved around a lot. The last place where I lived in a regular house was Jefferis with my Nanna. But my favourite was Mt Vickers. We were there three years, when I was a kid. Geez it was nice. Everyone was so friendly, and everyone knew everyone, and there was this huge lake where we went water-skiing and swimming. I often think about it. That was the happiest I've ever been.

The book with my story comes out about June. It's a long time to wait. It's going to be called *Bits and Pieces*, and it'll have stories and poems from all over. It'll be in hardback first, then paperback. Mrs McKinnon said I'll get a few free copies, but not many. I'll have to sign a contract, or some guardian'll have to sign it for me. Big time!

The money gets paid into a trust account. In other blocks you can have money — they get canteen twice a week — but not in A Block. We get a hand-out on Fridays — a choice of two blocks of chocolate or two packets of smokes. I usually have one of each. (But if you've been on PS that week you miss out.)

As for the story being true — yeah, most of it's true. Close enough. Blue's name wasn't Blue, he didn't have a bike, and he didn't have a gang, only me.

And I did write the poem on the birthday card. Glad you liked it.

OK, is that all? Can I go now? No, seriously, I don't mind you asking. Just as long as I can keep choosing which ones I answer.

Catch you later!
Love,
Trace

≈

Dear Trace,

Thanks for answering so many questions. I'm naturally inquisitive I guess. I don't mind if there's stuff you don't want to talk about. It's up to you.

But I tell you — I get so scared sometimes. What if I say the wrong thing? What if this gets messed up? And I tell you what scares me the most — all these dark hints you keep dropping about what you did to get put in there. I didn't know you'd be going on to the women's prison. That scares me. I guess you did do something pretty bad. You've never once hinted that you didn't do it, whatever it is — like, that you were innocent or anything. So where does that leave me? In a bit of a mess, still thinking that you're a friend, someone I trust (although you've given that a bit of a belting), someone who's basically, I dunno, good.

But maybe you're not. Maybe all my instincts are wrong, and they've been lying to me. I know I can't let myself believe that, otherwise the whole world falls apart and I've got nothing to hang onto. I have to keep believing in you or I can't believe in myself. I don't quite understand that, but I know it's true. I have to believe that if you did something awful it was because you were off your face or on drugs or you had an unhappy childhood or you were brainwashed in a cult or something. And, maybe most importantly, that now you're sorry you did it.

I don't mean, 'Sorry miss,' like you say at school, or sorry you got caught and got locked up for so long. I mean sorry deep inside you, so that you're a different person, better because of what you did. I know when you hurt someone you often can't repair the damage, so all you can do then is repair as much damage as you can, then go and do something in other areas to make up for it. Like, if I say something cruel to Mum, the way I do sometimes, so cruel that I know she'll never forget it, then I apologize as much as I can, then I go and clean up the garden or something.

I don't do it deliberately, it just happens that way. It's only while I've been writing this down that I've figured it out.

And — this is the big sentence now — you don't seem all that sorry when you write. Like you don't care much.

So here I am, what you once called a real person, living what you called a normal life, wondering how to manage with all this. I'm one of those kids the Human Dev. teacher last year politely called a 'late developer' (see, everyone's got a label for me), and sometimes it seems like a bit too much has happened in too short a time. Guess I just have to cope.

You know sometimes Mum says to me, 'Come on, Man, lighten up. You seem so gloomy nowadays.' And it's often after one of your letters. And in a way I wish I could be a happy innocent little kid again, putting my dolls to bed, telling Mum all the news from school, spending hours doing a beautiful heading for a project. But seems like everything's serious now — heavy stuff, grim stuff.

I used to look at those wrinkly lines on adults' foreheads and I thought they were so ugly, and Mum said they got them from worrying. So I thought 'OK, when I'm big and I get worried I'll keep my face smooth, and that'll save me getting wrinkles.' But now I realize it's not so easy.

You know the most frightening thing in my life is Steve, and if you were a true friend I'd be able to write to you about him, and you'd understand, and the way you wrote back would show that you understood. But you never wrote back that way. And since I found out you were in Garrett it's even harder to write about Steve. Why is that? I don't understand why that is.

Well, I was going to apologize for such a serious letter. But I'm not going to do that. To tell you the truth, while I've been writing it I've been thinking that I wouldn't send it. That gave me the courage to keep writing. But I will send it, I think, and without reading it back. That way I won't psych myself out again.

So — this is the end of the letter.

Be well,
Mandy

≈

Dear Mandy,

It's taken me a long time to answer your letter. I hope this time it'll work. All the previous attempts have ended in the bin.

When I started reading your letter I got so mad I could hardly finish it. I felt like you let me down. It was like you were lecturing me. I thought, 'Who the fuck is she, my rehab counsellor?' And it was like you were saying that I'm wrecking your life.

I got so mad I chucked your letter away. I wasn't going to write to you ever again.

Then, next morning, I was cleaning out my slot for inspection, the rubbish bag came round, and at the last minute I pulled your letter out. I thought maybe I might want to check up on something before I threw it out finally.

I kept it two days, then at the weekend I was so bored and mad with nothing to do that I read it again. It still got me fired-up, but at least when you're fired-up you know you're alive. And it was better than watching Anita Kelly swing her tits around the place.

But now, even now, this far into the letter, I'm stuck to know what to say. I don't want to lose you Mandy — you're my mate. People don't like me too much here. They're scared of me but they don't like me. It's hard to write this but it's true. And the thing is, I could say, 'Yeah, I'm sorry about what happened, about what I did, but it was basically Raz's fault and I didn't know it'd go as far as it did, I thought it was a joke at first, and yeah I was on the nod somewhat, as a matter of fact,' but the thing is Mandy, I don't want to suck you in any more, I want to keep it straight between us. And somehow I don't know what the truth is. You're confused? I'm confused. I don't know why I did it. You think I haven't thought about it? I've thought about it. And I still don't know.

And another thing is I don't know if I'm sorry or not. I'm too bloody mad to be sorry. I'm so burned-up at being in here I can't think sorry. I don't want to be in here. I want to be on a street. I want to be in a bus. I want to sit down the back of the bus and crack jokes and swap ciggies and stir the grannies and the gays and the drunks and the little kids. I want to eye off some hunk with an ass like a couple of rock melons. I want to turn on TV and watch any junk I want. I want to go out to this riding centre with a boyfriend I used to have and ride this beautiful big bay horse called Dillon, who always knew me and recognized me and remembered me. I want to know what happened to Marvin, my cat, the only pet I ever owned, and who's got him now, or whether they had him killed, or what happened.

I want to know where it all went wrong. How come I'm in here for four more years, when I should be having four years of freedom, being outrageous and jigging school and getting felt-up by guys and trying to decide if I should get a tat or not and having THE BEST YEARS OF MY

LIFE. Mandy, I came in here as a fucking fifteen-year-old and I'm gonna go out as a middle-aged fucking woman, just about ready to get married and have kids.

I know I should be sorry and I am, but then I start thinking about all this stuff and I get too confused and mad to be as absolutely truly sorry as I should be.

Well, I hope we can keep writing. But I'll understand if you don't want to. I'll hate it if you don't, I suppose I'll sort of hate you a bit, even though that's not fair to you. Not many people would have stuck on this long. So it's up to you. And if you want to write about Steve, write about him. I know I was stupid the way I ignored what you said before. But I've learnt a bit since then. I've met a few Steves in my time. I think Raz was a bit of a Steve — maybe that's another reason I didn't want to hear too much about your brother.

So, see you, be hearing from you, I hope.

Tracey

≈

November 14

Dear Trace,

Got your letter Monday; like you, I've spent a couple of days trying to write an answer.

Seems like each letter takes us a little further, you know what I mean? Not just in facts — like

94

your mentioning this guy Raz — but in the other ways too.

I do want to keep writing to you. The only thing I'm a bit scared of is that one day you'll break out of there and turn up on my doorstep in a stolen car wanting food and a bed and some plastic surgery. Or that you'll get out early because of some big reduction in your sentence and you'll want to move in and live with us and be my best friend. You see, I'm being honest again now, even though it hurts. I know the first one's not too likely but I guess the second one's possible. And what would happen if it turned out that you were 600 kilos and covered in tats, with a ring through your nose and all your teeth missing? OK, so I'm a snob, but I wouldn't like that. And my parents would freak out. They lead a quiet life.

Does this give you the shits? Am I just a snob? Got any answers?

Love,
Mandy

≈

Nov 18

Dear Mandy,

No, I don't think you're a snob. I was so scared when I came in here. Hope the hacks aren't reading this letter, 'cos I'd hate them to know that. But it's true. I thought they'd all be the biggest meanest

95

mothers in the valley — that's why I thought the only way to survive would be to be the biggest meanest mother of them all. And it wasn't that hard. A lot of them are real pussies in a clinch. But, yeah, sure, some of them are like you describe. Anita Kelly, whoo, 600 kilos did you say? Yeah, but her left boob's even bigger.

Seriously though, I don't know what to say. I don't blame you for being scared of me. I don't like it but I don't blame you. I'm scared of myself sometimes. Do we have to do a deal that I won't hassle you in four years? I will if you want, but it doesn't seem like much of a deal. Who knows where we're going to be, what we're going to be like, in four years? I've got a fair idea where I'll be, but you?

Don't think there's much we can do about it Manna, except to 'keep on goin' till it all stops flowin''.

A little black spider just ran across my desk. Geez he was moving. His feet hardly touched the ground. I used to hate spiders and cockroaches and stuff. I still don't much love 'em, but I don't mind them now, I don't kill them any more.

Shouldn't call this a desk. It's a metal table and chair all in one, cream-coloured, bolted to the floor near the front of the slot. Sitting here I can see most of A Block and a bit of sky. Three stars. A Block's a quadrangle. I'm in the bottom row, on the left as you come in, half-way along. The middle of the quadrangle's the exercise yard. Opposite me, on the bottom is the TV room, classrooms, showers and dunnies, and a storeroom. Above that are more slots. Above that's a kind of catwalk for the hacks. They just walk round and round trying to look like Dickless Tracy. They're all dykes anyway — for them the shower block's the sports and entertainment centre. You don't want to be too good-looking. There's one girl, Sophie, she's the one I get on best with I guess, when she takes a shower they swarm like flies at a funeral. I have to admit, she's got what it takes.

Well, I'm writing on about nothing. Ten minutes before lights out — I was going to do some homework and give Mrs McKinnon a shock. But one good thing about being in here, they don't expect anything. They pretend they do, and they go through their routines when we turn up empty-handed, but what can they do? Give us a detention? And they're sweating so hard to be positive, like they've been taught, they don't like to crack at us. The tutors that is; the hacks don't give a.

See you.
        Love,
            Trace

≈

November 22

Dear Trace,

I'm not going to pretend I want to swap places with you but your life is kind of . . . interesting? Sure is different to mine. Maybe you could write a book about it one day, make a million dollars.

97

Like I said before, I want to keep this going. It's gone too far to stop. It still scares me, but every day I come home I look to see if there's a letter from you. Jacinta, my 'pen pal' (hate that word), still writes occasionally, but it's not like this.

Your last letter was good. I could start to picture Garrett a bit. And I could picture you a bit too. You've never told me what you truly look like but it doesn't seem to matter so much these days. I'm still curious, but that's all it is now — curiosity.

Am I allowed to send you a Christmas present? I'd like to, but I don't know if you're allowed to get them. Please tell me.

Also, I'd like to tell Mum and Dad about you. I know they're not going to be thrilled, but I think I can make them understand. And if I don't tell someone, I'll burst. I feel like I'm carrying this dark secret around with me. I told Cheryl that we were writing again, and that you were a bit screwed-up (sorry!) and you were in a girls' home. She got quite into it — I think she thought it'd be like *Anne of Green Gables*. I wish!

You know, Sophie's the first person you've mentioned as a friend in there. Is she nice?

It seems so long since I wrote anything about me and my life — I'll have to start from scratch. Hope you can remember all the absorbing details. Right now we're burning up with tests and stuff. Kids like Rebecca are actually doing a bit of work. Mai Huynh's been round us too long — she's getting slacker. The worst ones are the teachers though. All the slack ones are going mad, giving us worksheets and revision hand-outs and tests. I think they're scared they'll get shown up when we fail. Or maybe they're worried they won't get the books finished.

I've noticed before though, everyone goes a bit mental at this time of year. Cheryl got busted a good one yesterday. She got Mrs Grogan's special chair, tied a bit of rope to it, and chucked it out the window — with a little help from her friends. (We were on the top floor.) Then she sat there holding the rope. Mrs Grogan came in, couldn't find the chair, made a big scene, wasted a quarter of an hour searching the building. She couldn't figure it out, she'd only been out of the room for three minutes, and it's a big chair. Not heavy, but big. Then the principal arrived. Bad luck for Cheryl, she'd been walking up the driveway, seen the chair hanging out the window. But she didn't say that at first. Just walked into the room and asked Cheryl to stand up. So Cheryl was well and truly gone. Mrs Grogan couldn't believe it — Cheryl's her star pupil. But like I said, everyone goes a bit mental at this time of the year.

Cheryl and Justin Smith (think I told you about him) are still a big double. She's lucky — he's sweet. They look good together — Cheryl's got beautiful brown skin and dark eyes and hair down to her waist. She dresses the best of anyone I know — I mean her family don't have heaps of money, but we go op-shopping, plus she makes quite a few things. Justin's tall, in fact he stoops a bit because I think he's self-conscious about his height. He's got brown hair and brown eyes and the whitest teeth — it's great when he cracks a smile. He dresses about the worst of anyone I know, but by the time Cheryl's finished with him he'll be doing ads for American Express, guaranteed.

Katrina's been home a lot lately. She's getting paranoid about her exams and says this is the only place she can study. All I can say is, it must be bad where she lives. She has big fights with Steve, usually about his music, which he wants to play full on. Heavy Metal, need I tell you? Steve's got a mate called Tim now, who's another fun guy: hasn't washed his hair since puberty; has a vocabulary of ten words, all obscene; thinks Rambo is a real person who's gonna call him up one day and invite him on a mission. Still, he keeps Steve off my back, 'cos Steve goes over to Tim's a lot. Thanks Tim, good buddy.

Mum and Dad are both working their lives away still. At least that's how it seems to me. They both say they enjoy their jobs but if you saw them when they get home you wouldn't think so. They're so short-staffed at the library that Mum and another lady are covering three jobs between them, and Dad works in theatres, where it's always high pressure. When they get home you wonder why they don't go back to Dad's hospital and have themselves admitted.

As for me, well, you remember Adam? You'd better remember Adam. Whatever happens I know I'm not going to forget him. I read this book the other day where all the girls kept talking about how they were in lust with different guys. Well, that's me I think, deeply in lust. And in love. Isn't it meant to be the girl who stops the guy from going too far? With us it seems like Adam's the only one with self-control. We were on a bus the other day, on opposite sides of the aisle, and I was looking at him and suddenly I wanted to throw myself at him, in front of all the people on the bus, and wrap myself around him. I had to hold onto the seat, I tell you.

Yeah, for once it's going well. Trouble is, I don't know what'll happen to us after next month. His final exams are on now and he finishes school December 7. Then he's working for his uncle (he's a builder) until uni starts — he wants to do law. He's a smart guy — I think he'll get in. He works hard too. He'd look cute in one of those wigs, walking down the street past the TV cameras, when he's defending someone famous.

Katrina's got a Christmas job in the post office, sorting mail, and she thinks she can get me in there in January, when the permanents are on leave, which'd be ace.

Anyway, I gotta fly. Mum's been hassling me for an hour to feed the dog, and now the dog's joining in. Abyssinia.

Mandy

≈

Dear Mandy,

Mandy, don't ever give me any shit about this place being interesting. It may sound that way to you, but you don't have to live here. For you, it's like watching a TV show or something. This place is a hole. It sucks, more than anything I'd ever imagined, and it's hard to stay cool when you write me a letter saying how good it all sounds.

Anyhow, I don't want to start another fight. I just got mad when I read your first paragraph. I'm coming up to the end of my fifteenth month, can you believe that? I came in here on September 1, the first day of spring. Very appropriate. I don't think it hit me till that day. At the remand centre they cushioned the shock. It was quite comfortable there, better than where I'd been living. And although I knew I couldn't walk out of the place I didn't understand what that meant till I got here. When the first lot of doors shut behind me, I realized I couldn't leave. That sounds stupid, but if you think about it, everywhere else you are in life, you can get out of it. If you don't like school you can jig it, if you don't like home you can piss off or go to a friend's place. But here, no matter what I did or said, no matter what I offered them, even if I slid on my stomach to their feet saying 'sorry' a thousand times, I still had to stay. That was bad.

And they set out to soften you up. In the paddy wagon they were telling me how I'd get bashed and raped and everything. This is the pigs, I mean. And when I got in here, it was the full routine: strip off, cavity searches, everything you own gets handed over. Then you've got to walk to the next room, in the nick, to get the uniform, while these pervs wet themselves watching you. And the uniform's such a winner: black shoes, khaki daks, white shirt, khaki jumper. At least they don't cut your hair any more.

Then I had to stand in this courtyard, with my feet on a white line, for about two hours, not allowed to move or talk. The shifts changed while I was there and one of the hacks, a young one, stopped and talked to me for a minute, then she was called away and I heard her getting told off! Can you believe it? I've never seen her since — she probably got the sack.

Then finally I got my stuff back — the bits I was allowed to keep — and got marched over to A Block, issued with toothpaste and junk, and put in my own little slot. My home away from home. And here I sit now, listening to the voices echoing round the quadrangle. It's about nine o'clock: we're not supposed to talk but it depends on who's on and how slack they are and how much noise you make. But you know, something strange happened a few minutes ago. You were asking about Sophie. Well, one thing Sophie can do is sing. And about a quarter of an hour ago when it was quiet — no-one was talking or anything — she started singing 'Missing, Maybe Lost'. You know it?

'When you're in love
And when you're lonely,
And he's gone, you don't know where.
You start thinking
You're the only
One who ever, seems to care.
And you look round every corner,
You're afraid to leave the phone.
You have joined the nothing army
Of the lost and the alone.'

Well, she sang it, and I swear to God no-one moved
in this whole block, not even the hacks. It was
like the world stopped. It was so still: no wind,
no noises, just this voice. Then after she finished,
you could hear people crying. Not me, I don't cry,
they call me Ice-eyes, but some people were. And
it's funny, although they're talking again now, it's
different — everyone's so quiet.

   Soph's amazing. They call me Ice-eyes, but they
call her Bedroom-eyes. She's in for RWV, like most
of A Block. To look at her you wouldn't think
she'd walk on the grass without permission. You
asked, 'Is she nice?' Jeez Mandy, no offence, but
I really laugh at some of the things you say. Nice!
No-one's fucking nice in here. But I talk to her
a bit. I'm not sure what a friend is any more, but
she's the closest thing to one that I've got. See,
in here, it's all groups, everyone hangs round in
groups, for protection mainly, but a few of us keep
to ourselves. I'm one and Soph's another. Some
do it because they're pussies, some do it 'cos

no-one wants them, some do it 'cos they're off their trollies. I do it 'cos it makes me stronger. I don't know why Soph does it — I can't make her out.

It's funny, I don't care about being top dog any more, and when Anita came in, all hot to take over, I wasn't going to stand in her way. And she was doing OK too, scoring a few points. But she's so stupid, she should have left me alone. She started hassling me to get out of the showers a few days ago, and I dropped her with a backhander through the nose. Fair dinkum, I've never hit anyone so hard. Her head bounced into the wall and she went down screaming, like a beached whale, blood everywhere. She just went too far. Anyway, I've written a poem about her:

> There was a young slag called Anita,
> Who thought nobody could beat her.
> Until she met Trace,
> And got hit in the face,
> And now she couldn't be sweeter.

Pretty good, eh? Raz taught me how to fight. He said, go for the nose, and try to put their nose through the back of their head, don't stop till you feel air on the other side. But he was bloody frightening in a fight. He went psycho.

Anyhow I didn't mean to write all this. I try not to write the bad stuff, about me or this place, but it slips in.

Oh yeah, one last thing, I don't care about Christmas and that junk but the rules are that you can send me parcels any time. They get opened and searched. If it's legal stuff I can have it; if it's illegal (I mean, things I can't have in my slot) I get it when I finally go out. By which time it mightn't be good for much. You can't send food — don't know what happens if you do, imagine the hacks eat it.

As for telling your parents, that's up to you. It's not going to make much difference to me. But what if they stop you writing? Or want to read my letters or something?

Hey that was a good story about Cheryl and the chair. I liked that. And Adam sounds a bit of a winner. If you want to send a real Christmas present, send him in for a few days. I'm getting desperate. Next time they give us bananas for fruit I won't be responsible for what happens.

Geez I can't believe how long these letters are getting. I'm quitting this right here. See you.

Love,
Tracey

≈

November 25

Dear Trace,

Well, I did tell my parents. Tonight actually, without waiting for a letter from you. I just thought it was the right thing to do. It was a difficult scene. I'm not very good at those 'let's sit down and have a family discussion' situations. Just getting Mum and Dad together without Steve and Katrina wasn't easy. But after tea on Saturday Steve was doing a bit of work (too little, too late) and Katrina was doing a lot of work and Mum and Dad were watching TV. I had to wait for the commercials, then it went something like this. (Well, you said you wanted to hear about a real family!)

'Um, hey, you know Tracey, who's been writing to me?'

Mum: 'Yes.'

Dad: 'Nuh, who's Tracey.'

Me: 'Oh Dad, you know. She put that ad in *G.D.Y.*'

Dad: 'Nuh.'

·Me: 'And I answered her ad, and we've been, like, pen pals all year.'

Dad: 'Oh yeah?'

Me: 'Well, I thought I'd better tell you a few things... it hasn't quite worked out the way I thought it would.'

At this point Mum realizes that something fairly heavy could be going down, so she starts paying more attention to me than the TV.

Mum: 'What do you mean?'

Me: 'Well, I thought she was a normal kid, OK, looking for someone to swap letters with...'

Mum: 'Yes?'

Me: 'But it turns out she's in Garrett.'

Dad, sitting up: 'You mean, Garrett, where they put the girls... the ones who've been in court?'

Me: 'Yeah.'

Mum: 'But you mean she's been there all along? And you didn't know?'

Me: 'Yeah. I didn't know at first. But she told me a while ago.'

Dad: 'How could you not know?'

Me: 'Well, I was writing to a post-office box. And she was writing like she was in a normal family.'

Pause. They're trying to figure out what line to take.

Dad: 'Well, what's she in for?'

Me: 'I dunno. She won't tell me.'

Now they start to bubble, and the steam's not far away. I gotta act fast.

Me: 'But it's OK. She doesn't have to tell me. I like writing to her, and they're the only letters she gets.'

Mum: 'But what happens when she gets out?'

Me: 'Well, she won't, not for a long time.'

Dad: 'How long?'

Me: 'Four years.'

Dad: 'Four years! I don't like the sound of that. She's not there for jaywalking.'

Me: 'I don't care. It doesn't matter to me.'

No-one knows what to say.

Dad: 'I don't know what to say.'

Me: 'Well, I thought you should know.'

Dad: 'Maybe we should contact the place, Garrett, and ask them about it. Get their advice.'

Me: 'No! No way! Don't you dare do that. She's my friend, and I'm going to keep writing to her no matter what, and I don't want her to think I'm spying on her.'

Mum: 'Well what do you want us to do then?'

Me: 'I just thought you should know.'

Mum: 'Well I'm glad you did. I'm glad you told us. And it says a lot for you that you've been loyal to this girl.' (Sorry Trace.) 'But naturally we're worried about how it's come about. It doesn't sound like she's been too honest with you.'

Me: 'No she wasn't at first. I think she is now.'

Dad's been sitting there for a while, not saying anything. Now he suddenly stirs into action, like he's made a big decision. 'Mandy, none of the kids know this, but maybe I ought to tell you.'

Me (scared): 'Tell me what?'

Dad: 'When I was a kid I got put in one of those places for six weeks. I was only 15, but I'd been truanting a lot, and I'd been warned a few times. Then I got caught knocking off bikes and selling them. So in I went.'

At this point Mandy falls to the ground in a dead faint. No she doesn't, but it's only her amazing self-control that saves her. My dad in a kind of Garrett? Or Ruxton, I should say? This is about the most amazing thing that's ever happened in our family.

Anyway, as time goes on the full story comes out. He went to a training farm in the country for his six weeks. It was probably mild compared to your A Block but he said it was horrible and he hated every minute of it. He said he only got one letter a week, from his mum, and letters mean so much in those places that if I'm the only one writing to you, I'd better keep writing. But he also said that some of the people in there are hopeless cases and he doesn't want to make me a suspicious type of person, but I should be careful.

So, there it is. I've always tried to be honest with you and so I swear that this is a true and honest account of our conversation, for better or for worse.

Mandy

≈

November 29

I didn't send that stuff from Saturday yet, 'cos I figured there'd be a letter from you about now, and there it was today.

Look, I'm sorry about saying Garrett sounded interesting. Did I really say that? That wasn't one of my best efforts. And I'd like to lend you Adam for a while but they might confiscate him — I guess he's a perishable, like a food item. Good enough to eat. But I will send you a Chrissie pressie.

The mighty Mum's Army softball team's back in action, with a few new members. We had training this afternoon. Sheez, what a squad. We've got this new pitcher, Louisa, when she walks on the field it tilts in her direction. Awesome. Only trouble is she pitches ten balls for every strike. We've entered D Grade this season — that's the lowest — but I don't think we'll rewrite any record books.

The only other big news is that Rebecca's leaving. She lives with her mum, and her mum's a primary teacher, and she's been transferred to Salter's Wall. They're leaving after Christmas. Funny, I think I'll miss Rebecca. As a friend, she's like Louisa as a pitcher, ten balls for every strike. Still, she's been around so long now. It'll be strange without her.

I gotta go. Thanks for your letter. Parts of it were quite stunning actually. I'm nervous about how you'll react to the stuff with my parents, but I'm determined to send it.

> Lots of love,
> *Mandy*

≈

Dec 3

Dear Mandy,

God I get sick of starting every letter the same way. So boring. But I'm in such a bad mood. Or maybe good and bad. I'm sick, got a middle ear infection and general flu and stuff. Got put in Med Unit yesterday, am still here, and writing this sitting in bed. So I feel lousy. But you do get looked after better here, especially times like now, when they're not busy. Matron says I'm run down, gotta look after myself. She hasn't told me how though.

I went on sick parade Saturday, with a sore ear and they poked around in it and said it was OK. Then when I woke up Sunday morning there was blood all over my pillow. It gave me a hell of a shock. And I felt generally crook. So that's how I ended up in here.

The good news is that the food's better, you get to watch a lot of TV, and some of the staff are half-way human.

Thanks for your letter. You know, you're the most reliable person I've ever met. Not that I've met you. I don't mind about your telling your parents — they sound cool. That's amazing about your father. Remember ages ago I was telling you how Roy Lugarno, out of Dust and Ashes, had been in Ruxton? Seems like people do survive. There is life after death.

You see Manna I don't think I'll survive this place, either this place or Macquarie. I try to imagine myself walking out free, in the open air, but even though I think I've got a good imagination there's no picture when I press that particular button. I think I'll die in here, I often think that.

Oh well, better not rave on. Sorry this is a short letter, by our standards anyway, but I do feel shitty. I don't know whether I want to get out of Med Unit or not. I don't think I do. Hope A Block's holding together without me. Anita'll be happy anyway. Matter of fact I imagine most people will be.

See you.
From your sickening mate,
Trace

≈

Dear Manna,

That was pretty nice of you. I got the biggest shock. That's the first phone message I've had in Garrett, not counting the one Mrs Neumann may or may not have had. How'd you find the number? I think it's right at the front under Government Departments. Everyone says that people outside can never find it.

There's a lot of rules about phone messages that I didn't bother to tell you, because I didn't think you'd be needing to know. It's meant to be only your parents, and only messages of information, like 'We can't come this weekend.' For birthdays they sometimes bend the rules. But I suppose because I'm sick they let this one through. Also because it was Miss Gruber (the hack you spoke to), and she's nicer than most of them. I asked her what you sounded like and that surprised her, 'cos I haven't been talking to hacks much. But she said you sounded nice and that you were worried and everything. I mean, I'm not dying; in fact I'm much better.

But thanks, OK?

I'm still in Med Unit, as you've probably figured out. If I'd been the bitch I usually am they'd have sent me back by now, but I'm being a try-hard at the moment, helping make beds and wash dishes and sort linen. Sunshine's my middle name. So they love me here and they'll probably adopt me and keep me forever.

Actually I'm still feeling lousy. I hate being sick, it's so depressing.

I just read your message again, and you know Manna, I fucking love you. Not like a lemon or anything. I just do.

Hey your softball team sound like they need a bit of confidence. You gotta start the season thinking Grand Final. I'm not just spinning on here: in my past life, before I came back as a slag, I won a few things. High-jumping, mostly. I cleared 1.53 when I was 13. If the walls in this place were a fraction lower I'd flop right over them. The broken glass would be a worry though.

OK, end of transmission. Sayonara,

Trace

December 6

Dear Tracey,

Well, just spent half an hour fighting my way through the Garrett telephone system. It's worse than ringing Mum at work. In fact it was unbelievable. Anyway, I finally got through to a lady who sounded OK (sorry if she's the biggest bitch in the place) and she said she'd bend the rules and make sure you got the message. We had a good goss actually. She kept saying how she wasn't allowed to discuss 'the girls' then she'd spend five minutes

114

talking about you. I hope she doesn't get into trouble.

She said you'd been 'very difficult', but you were 'much nicer lately'. Sounds like you're the big improver Trace. Way to go.

Anyway, hope you're over the flu. I hate being sick — I become a vegetable when I am — want to crawl under the bed and stay there till I get better. Like my dog. When I was 11 I had rubella so badly, then the day before I was due to go back to school I said to Mum: 'What are these little red spots on me, Mum?' It was chickenpox. This year the worst thing's been period pains — I've had some tough days.

I'd like to get glandular fever, like Rebecca. It seems like such a slack disease. You lie around doing nothing, all day every day.

Tomorrow's when Steve and Adam finish their school careers. Historic moment. I'm happy for Adam 'cos he's escaping at last (he's been hanging out for it for so long); jealous, 'cos it's him, not me; scared, about what'll happen to our relationship; and sad, 'cos I know I won't see as much of him next year. As for Steve, I don't have any feelings. I honestly can't see how he could possibly get much. And no employer would want him — they can breed their own rats. So if he doesn't get into a course and he can't get a job, what's going to happen? He's going to hang around here all day, that's what. Think I might tunnel into Garrett and share a room with you.

He even said the other day that he might repeat

Year 12, but Mum and Dad jumped on that fast.

He's so pathetic. You almost feel sorry for him. There's heaps of parties on this weekend — you can imagine — and he sits around talking about what a rage it's going to be, and how he's going to get wasted, but I know he hasn't got an invitation to any of them, except an official one that everyone's invited to.

We had softball training again tonight. I often seem to write to you on Thursdays. In fact I hardly plan to do homework on Thursdays, I'm so busy writing these letters. Anyway training went better. For me it sure did — I hit the sweetest shot I've ever hit — it went a kilometre beyond second base. It felt magic. But what worries me is, if I do that against Louisa (she's our new pitcher), what could a good batter do? For example, the batters in all the teams we play against this season.

Wonder if it's too late to switch to ten-pin bowling?

Listen, if you could spend a perfect day, how would you spend it? Cheryl asked me that. I think for me it'd be to sit on top of this mountain we did a school hike to last year, and read books and eat chocolate all day, with no interruptions. Mt Cobbler it was. No matter what direction you looked, you couldn't see any evidence of humans, except one huge area that the loggers had bulldozed so they could fish out their logs. It made me sick to see it, when everything else was so beautiful. I've been a lot more careful with timber and paper since then. Maybe we should write shorter letters.

Maybe I better finish this one before going on to a new page.

Take lots of care Trace,
                    Your mate,
                         Mandy

≈

                                   Dec 10

Dear Mandy,

Well, I'm out of Med Unit, back to normal life. Normal? Ha! Life? Ha! Didn't go to any classes or anything today, couldn't be bothered. You don't have to go if you don't want to so I did nothing. No, that's not true, I did do something. I smoked — half a packet. Doesn't leave much for the rest of the week.

You know how in movies everyone breaks out of these places? I honestly don't see how they could. Hacks are up above, watching all the time. Tunnels aren't the go — don't want to wreck my fingernails. The only way I can think of is to smash a window, grab some glass, hold it to a hack's throat and invite her to lead me to the front gate. I'd do it too. Hello to any hacks reading this.

I had a good time this morning, carving Anita's name into a chair in the common room. Set her up nicely. Then I had a good time this afternoon carving my own name into my arm with a big paper clip that I'd sharpened up a bit. Wish I'd sharpened it up more though.

117

Manna you really give me the shits with some of your questions. I mean, I've said all this before but you keep doing it. And that dumb joke about tunnelling in here.

You want to know what my perfect day would be? It'd be to get a machine gun and walk through here spraying the whole place with so much lead they could have a new floor. A lead-lined floor, with red colouring.

You know what my perfect day would be, you didn't have to ask. To have a mum who you could sit down and talk to about school and boys and stuff, and then you'd muck around with your sister for a while and try on all her clothes, and then you'd give your brother some advice about his girlfriend, then you'd go out and play with your cat in the sun. Just all that sort of shit.

Do you know Sophie didn't come and see me once when I was in Med Unit? Even though it's easy to do — you go on sick parade and sneak in while you're waiting. I went and saw her twice when she had her wisdom teeth out.

I couldn't sleep last night. Nearly started writing you a letter in the middle of the night.

Sorry I'm in such an off mood.

Tracey

≈

Dear Mandy,

Ignore yesterday's letter. I'm still as raggy as hell but why should you suffer? I got two days PS last night, for yelling 'fuck off' at a hack when she told me to sandpaper yesterday's graffiti. And someone got into my room and pissed on my bed — probably Anita.

Soph got busted with some bombers this morning so it's all happening here. Searches everywhere. Dunno how she got them but it's not hard. Christ, she's dumb though — she had them in a little plastic pill bottle with her name on it, in case she lost them. Can you believe it? Good bust, Soph.

I gotta see the shrink tomorrow, don't know why. Should be good for a laugh.

See you,
        Trace

≈

Dec 12

Dear Mandy,

Daily letters. Hope you're grateful. I've got nothing much to do at the moment, so thought I might as well write again. Not that there's anything to write about. School's stuffed — I haven't been going to many classes. It's all slack anyway 'cos it's the end of year, and most of the tutors are leaving. They can't take the pace.

Saw the shrink today. She said I should go on a thing called the Anger Control Programme. These names, fair dinkum, they've got a name for everything.

I think I control my anger pretty well. I control it so well no-one even knows I'm angry. Until I explode like World War Three, that is. Then they have a fair idea.

I don't think the shrink thought that was such a hot method though.

The thing is Manna — and don't dare tell anyone this — I'm kind of caught. Because of what Raz and I did, I know I don't deserve any sympathy. And if my smokes get knocked off, or a hack gives me PS or NP (no privileges) for something I didn't do, or I start thinking about all the things I'm missing out on, then yeah, I get mad. I get so mad I want to scream and bite and kick and tear this place to pieces. I want to get on top of that wall and rub myself in the broken glass. But as soon as I start getting mad, a little voice inside me says 'How can you complain? After what you did? You've got no right.' And so I stop myself. I think 'No matter how tough I've got it, I'm better off than...' I don't want to finish that sentence but you get the drift.

It gets me confused.

Sorry to keep hitting you with depressing letters. All I seem to be able to do at the moment is write to you. Don't worry though. I'm cruising.

Catch you later

Trace

≈

120

Dear Trace,

Gee the letters are flooding in suddenly. But they
don't add up to too good a picture. You sound
like you're off the rails Trace. What's happening?
Is there anything I can do? I don't think I've ever
been this helpless in my life.

It seems so trivial to write about anything here
while you're getting bruised around. Most of what
happens in Acacia Park is trivia, except that today
we finished school at last. It's been a long term. I
can't believe I'm heading for Year 11. When I think
how scared and envious I was of those big girls on
the bus... but now I'm there I don't feel too enor-
mous, and my friends don't look so old either.

I thought we'd have a wild end-of-year but it
was quite flat. I was too tired to celebrate. A few
people tried to work up some action but not much
happened. There is a party tonight though, at Paul
Bazzani's — think I'll go when I've finished this.
Last weekend was fairly wild, with all the Year
12 turns. Adam's been walking around in a coma
ever since.

Tomorrow's our first softball game. Mum's
Army is playing in a holiday comp., so we can
be full on for the big time in February.

Anyway, think I'll go. My heart's not in this
— I'm too worried about what's happening with
you. I don't want to tell you what I think you
should do — how can I, when you're the one who
has to live in that place? But Trace, please be

careful. Can't you cut back a bit? Tread softly for a while? Let Anita take over if she wants? I know it's easy for me to say this but I'd hate to see you get into any more trouble.

Take care — be well,

Love,
Mandy

≈

Dec 14

Dear Manna,

Just a note — one of the nurses said she'd post it, so you should get it sooner than usual. Anyway I thought I'd tell you I'm back in Med Unit, not for anything in particular. They just want to keep an eye on me or something. So, hope you're well and having a good weekend.

Love,
Tracey

≈

December 18

Dear Tracey,

Hope you got my messages — I rang twice, in case one didn't get through. I'm getting better at the phone system. I've found out there's a direct number to the Med Unit, so it's easier.

The second time I got that nice one again, Miss Gruber. I thought I'd rung A Block somehow, but she said she was there to take sick parade. We had another goss. Don't get me wrong, I didn't say much, 'cos I know that's the way you'd want it. I'm not about to start blabbing to them about you. But you did say she was one of the nicer ones.

Anyway, she asked how I knew you, and I said only through letters, and that we write all the time. And she said 'Well you must know her well by now.' And I said 'Yes, she's about my best friend I guess.' And she said 'Well, she needs her friends.' And I said 'How is she?' and she said 'Depressed.' And I said 'I wish I could help.' And she said 'Well, keep writing. If I think of anything more practical, I'll give you a call.' So she took my name and number, as well as the message for you. Don't imagine anything'll come of it, but at least she seems to care.

But you know Trace, thinking about it later, I'm not so sure about this best friend stuff. Sometimes it seems like you're not that interested in my life. Especially Steve. I don't write about him much nowadays — I'm still sensitive about it. But a real friend would try and help more, wouldn't she? This last week Steve's been out of control. I think he's scared about his results. But I'm scared of him. He slaps me, knees me, kicks me. I lock my door quite often when I'm in my bedroom now, that's how much he scares me.

I suppose being in a place like Garrett must

make you selfish in a way, because there's only you to concentrate on.

Don't take all this the wrong way. I do feel close to you — that's the only reason I can say these things. I think true friends keep pushing each other up the ladder — they don't just sit about at the same level.

Keep on keeping on,
M.

≈

Dec 19

Dear Manna,

I'm still shaking, and grinning like an idiot. It's only five minutes since I hung up. That was the biggest shock I've had in this place.

You know, that Miss Gruber, I was such a bitch to her last week. I called her every name you can think of, plus a few they don't have at Acacia Park. It was because she turned the TV off two minutes before the end of 'Hotel for Strangers'. I know it's not that great a show but I wanted to see the end. Anyway, I'm embarrassed about it now.

So, how'd you think I sounded, huh? Dumb for the first five minutes, I bet. I nearly lost my voice. When she gave me the phone, I thought it'd be the shrink, 'cos she said she'd ring Matron this afternoon to see how I was. Then this little voice said 'Tracey? It's Mandy.' I just sat there with my mouth open. Every time I tried to say something I had to cough instead. Words wouldn't come out. Must have sounded great to you, but my throat went all tight and sore. And when I could speak I couldn't think of anything to say at first.

Manna, I don't understand why you're so good to me, when I lied to you and all that.

Anyhow, once my throat unlocked and I warmed up a bit, it was great. In fact I felt like I was gabbling, the words came so fast. Hope you didn't mind. I'm not normally like that, but it was the first time in over a year I felt free to talk. I couldn't believe it when they said it was half an hour and I had to stop. Seemed like five minutes.

That was good about your softball. Unbelievable in fact. The way you wrote about them, I thought they'd be more like Grandma's Army than Mum's. And I don't care what you wrote in your letter, I won't be offended. Hope it comes tomorrow but.

Manna, you sound so cool. A sort of laughing, happy voice, nervous at first, but then all husky and nice. Not like anyone in here. They all start to sound the same after a while.

Well, I've got to finish this, 'cos the nurse who's posting it is going off in a minute. See you!

Heaps of love,
Ice-eyes

≈

Dear Trace,

God, that was exciting. I was so nervous, but once we got going it was great. That silence after I said who I was — I thought it'd last forever. And when you said 'Mandy?' you sounded like some ninety-year-old. But by the end I couldn't get a word in edgeways. I'm glad though, 'cos Miss Gruber said you hadn't said anything much for weeks. I didn't realize you were so, you know, out of it. You should have told me.

Ignore what I said in my last letter about being selfish — it was just an impulse.

I never thought Miss Gruber would do anything, when she took my number. I nearly died when she rang this afternoon. But the thing I was scared of was that we wouldn't be able to talk — that there'd be this long painful silence, then we'd start discussing the weather. I thought it was a big gamble, 'cos it could have wrecked the whole thing. But I also knew that once she'd offered, I had to accept.

So how'd I sound, huh? Sexy voice? You were totally different to what I expected. I thought your voice would be really tough and rough. But you sound so cute. That's probably an insult in A Block. You sounded like a Sunday School student giving another right answer. It makes me more curious to see what you look like.

You know, we're heading for our first anniversary. Amazing, hey?

Anyway, get out of the Med Unit fast. And then, why don't you put in a bit of a try-hard effort and get transferred to an easier block? Is that possible? I reckon you should go for it.

Love always,
M.

≈

Dear Manna,

Well, the letter you'd warned me about turned up today. It wasn't so bad, but thanks for the warning. I deserve everything you said. Of course this place makes you selfish — you've gotta be, or you're dead. Trust no-one, get everything you can for yourself — that's how it works. After a while you think about yourself so much — how to get more food, more smokes, longer showers; how to stop people hassling you; how to get the best jobs. And you get sick of everyone whingeing all the time and telling the same stories over and over, so you think about yourself even more.

I suppose they encourage it in a way, with the shrinks and all that. It's got its good points but. I've learnt a bit about myself.

As for Steve ... well, I've tried to say this before. I guess I owe it to you to spell it out. You see Manna, I know there are good families out there. I've heard about them and I've seen them from a distance. And they fascinate me. One of the things I hoped when I put the ad in was to get closer to one of those families, kind of get inside one. Not that it was any huge deal — I'd forgotten about the ad five minutes after I sent it off. I never paid for it either — I couldn't. I got threatening letters from them for months. Wonder what they planned to do — arrest me?

Anyhow, when you started dropping hints about an off brother I was curious, of course. So I pestered you to tell me. But when you did, I felt sick. It was like the same old thing again — violence. I felt like I'd been born into that, grown up in it, breathed it and eaten it. I needed to know that there were families where it didn't happen; I didn't need to know about another one where it did. Now I'm on the verge of going further than I meant to; further than I should. I can feel it. If you've got any sense Manna, don't read on. No, I'm not about to tell you my life story — I don't think I could ever do that. But I'll tell you a chapter or two. And like I said, be smart and stop reading now.

OK, if you're still reading, you asked for it. I know now my father was what they call violent. I've only realized that lately. We never thought of him that way; we didn't have names for it. Sometimes he'd be angry and he'd hit us and we'd be scared and try and keep out of the way, and we'd walk quietly and talk quietly. Stay in our bedrooms. See what I mean? Like if someone's an alcoholic, their kids probably wouldn't think that, they'd just hate it when their Mum or Dad was drunk. You don't think of it as a condition or an illness or anything. And we were only little.

And yeah, he'd hit Mum and we'd hate that and cry and try to fight him off. Just like you see in the movies. I've had to walk out of some movies, like *Abbie* and *Cry Baby Cry*.

By the way another thing I've never told you. There were only two of us kids. My brother, Simon, who's three years older, and me. The only relatives we had were Nanna, who was Mum's mum, and an aunt and uncle in Scotland, who I don't know much about. I don't remember Mum's dad. Dad's parents died when he was little, and he was brought up by an uncle.

Anyhow, one day when I was about eight, Nanna suddenly told me I'd be living with her for a while. I was quite pleased, but a bit puzzled. I remember asking her if Simon was coming too, and she said no, which I thought was strange.

Nanna was old then, so it wasn't as much fun living there as I thought it would be. After a while — could have been a couple of months, I can't remember — I asked if I could go back home. That's when she told me that my Mum had died and my Dad had gone away. And when I said 'What about Simon?' she said he was being looked after by some other people.

It didn't sink in for a while, but when it did I started to go a bit funny, I think. I don't remember that period clearly but I know I did some stupid things, like sleeping under the bed, and crapping in cupboards at school. I always seemed to be in trouble, which was a good joke, because I'd been one of those super-suction kids up till then. Never went over the lines when I was colouring-in.

Anyhow, I got worse and worse. I ended up known as the local slut, head-banger, low-life, all of which didn't bother me. But the good thing was, Nanna didn't know much about it. She was pretty weak by then and couldn't do much for herself. And I kept getting quite good marks, without doing any work.

Then one day I came home real late and she wasn't there. I was so scared. Then the lady next door came in and told me Nanna had been knocked over by a boy on a bike and had her hip broken and was in hospital. But this lady didn't waste any words telling me — she thought I was such a hard case that I didn't deserve any consideration. What the hell, she was probably right.

She sure hung it on me for being so late home though. See the thing was, if I'd been there on time, I'd have gone to the shops instead of Nanna and the accident would never have happened. Any kid tried to run me over, I'd be wearing his balls around my neck on his bike chain.

Well then it went pretty much like in that story I sent you. When she came out of the operation Nanna was a space case, and after a while she died. I knew I had to get out of town fast then, or Community Services would get me. I'd cleaned the whole house up while Nanna was sick, so it was easy to pack what I wanted. I rang Raz, then got clothes and money and food and stuff, and put it all in a couple of bags.

Then I got some papers out of the bottom of Nanna's wardrobe, where I'd seen them while I was tidying up. They were these envelopes, stuck up tight with sticky tape. They were the only papers in the house. I'd been hoping they were money. I didn't touch them while Nanna was alive,but now that she was dead I thought it'd be all right. So I opened them.

It was just newspaper clippings, so I was disappointed. But I flicked through them anyhow. Then I saw a photo of my father. I recognized him straight away, even though it had been so long. The headline said 'Police Praised In Murder Trial.' I thought maybe my father had been a policeman, which surprised me a lot. Then I started reading the article and found it was my father who'd done the murder. Then I read a bit further and found he'd got 18 years. Then I read to the end and found it was my mother who he'd murdered.

A bit later Raz came round with his panel van and we went up north.

I still don't know where Simon is. And I don't know where my father is — probably still in the Q. Although 18 years never means what it says.

Anyhow, wherever he is, I guess he'd be proud of me, following in his footsteps. Seems like some things do run in the family.

All I can say, Manna, is I hope you stopped reading back on the first page, like I told you.

See you,
     Tracey

≈

Dear Manna,

Just to tell you that the parcel got here. God you're a dickhead, but thanks a lot. I asked them not to give it to me till Christmas Day: if there's anything illegal in it there's more chance of getting it on Christmas Day. It's a good time for bargaining.

This'll be my second Christmas in here. Last year wasn't too cheerful — a girl offed herself on Christmas morning. She did it with one of those flex cords from an electric jug, that she'd knocked off from the dining hall.

No-one gets too excited about Christmas here, though a lot of them have visitors. The food's good though.

Time's passing slowly at the moment. You don't like classes much when they're on, but they leave a hole when they finish. We've invented this new game called Points. There's a few little balls of Blu-tack around, each one with a drawing pin in it, right? (Both the Blu-tack and the drawing pins are illegal, needless to say.) And whoever's got one hangs onto it until she sees a good target — another slag, that is. When you see someone you chuck it at them as hard as you can, so it sticks in them. If they cry out, or make any sound at all when it hits, they lose a point. If they stay silent they get a point.

Some people are on minus five already. Ice-eyes here's on plus three and going nowhere but up.

Well, it helps fill in the hours.

I'm reading this book at the moment called *A Place Like Home*. It's by this woman who was brought up in an orphanage in Sydney, in the 1920s, with her sisters. Geez it'd break your heart. What those kids went through. The way they got treated, you wouldn't think anyone would get away with it. When they went on a holiday, just once in their little lives, it was like they'd been given the universe.

It's a true story and I swear Manna, you'd love it. You ought to try and get a copy.

Hope this arrives by Christmas. If so, have a really good time, OK? Get into the grog, pig out on the food, make Adam crawl for everything he gets, and think of me.

Happy Christmas.

Love,
    Tracey

≈

Dear Trace,

Got your letter a few minutes ago — funny it was so like mine. I'm glad you liked talking — like I said, it seemed such a massive risk. But I still smile when I think about it. And thanks for what you said about my voice.

Think I told you most of my news on the phone. We're having a party for Rebecca New Year's Eve, a farewell. It's at Angelo Bouras' — he's been with Becca for quite a while. In fact he'll be cut to ribbons when she leaves.

Cheryl, Mai Huynh and I went round the seconds shops yesterday. I got this great outfit at Battle of the Sexes: you can get some good stuff there, but it's still expensive. Buying that, plus all the Christmas shopping, has cleaned me out — hope I score some cash for Chrissie. And I'm still hoping to get a job mail-sorting in January, but Katrina said they don't confirm it till about two days before you start. Dad's working a late on Christmas Day, so we'll go to Midnight Mass Christmas Eve and have Christmas dinner early: about 11.30 or 12. It'll only be like half a Christmas Day really. But it should be fun. All the rellies are coming over Boxing Day, including the lovely Uncle Kevin and Aunty Sophie, and Justin the Dentist. I'm hoping Adam will come too, meet the in-laws, ha ha. Or if he can't come here I'll try to go there, although the way my parents are about family reunions, if I do go I'll probably never be allowed back home again.

That's a joke by the way.

I gotta tell you too that Steve's getting so weird even Mum and Dad are having to face the fact. They're talking about his seeing a shrink, but no-one's talking about it to him yet. He spends most of his time in his room reading gun magazines, and when he talks to anyone it's only a mutter, or it's some riveting comment about a new Canadian howitzer that disembowels babies or something. He used to have this mate Tim, but when I asked about Tim the other day he went sick at me and told me to shut my fucking mouth, and said I'd been talking to Tim about him and how it was Tim's fault he was going to fail Year 12. It was weird. I think he's heading for the drop zone. What really scares me is that he's got this .22 and a shotgun that Grandpa left him. He uses them for rabbit-shooting, although he hasn't been for a while. But he spends a lot of time cleaning the guns and taking them apart.

I wish Mum and Dad would take them off him. I think they're illegal anyway — aren't you meant to have a licence?

Anyway I'd hate to be in a McDonalds if he walks in one day.

So, this'll be the last letter from me before Christmas. That's if it gets there in time. It should though — Katrina was saying how they have extra deliveries before Christmas, and two on Christmas Eve. Trace, I know Garrett on Christmas Day isn't likely to be the happiest place on the planet but I hope it's a good day anyway. Hope my parcel gets there too. Lots and lots of love and hugs, for a good Christmas and even better New Year,

Your friend,
Manna

PS: Mum just came home, and she said to say Merry Christmas to you too. She paid the postage on the parcel, and she said she snuck some chocolate in.

≈

Dec 25

Dear Manna,

I'm not very good at thanking people but maybe that's one of the things I need to learn. So here goes. Thanks for the presents — I can keep everything. The pen's fantastic — so good. I'll have to guard it with my life here, I swear. And the soap smells so great I don't want to use it — I'll keep it just for the smell. And they let me have the chocolate — I told you this is the best day for sleazing. Please tell your Mum thanks from me. And also, thanks for the Christmas letter, which came yesterday. And finally, thank you for being such a good friend all year. I didn't know what I was getting when your first letter came, but it's really been something.

To tell you the truth, I hate being in anyone's debt. I hate it. But if I've got to owe anyone favours, I'd just as rather it was you. And one day maybe I'll get the chance to pay you back — I hope so.

The bad news is that Miss Gruber's been transferred, to Abbotsville I think. She came round Saturday to say goodbye. She was quite burned-off that they gave her no warning, but that's the way they seem to do it round here.

So, Chrissy in Garrett's nearly over. Yes folks, another great one, filled with goodwill and cheer. It wasn't too bad I suppose. The food was good, and heaps of it. I ate all day. And we could watch TV as much as we wanted, although there wasn't anything good on. Nothing else happened, just some stupid jokes and games. There was a good fight between two girls: Kylie Patrick and a girl called Turk. I don't know her real name. The hacks broke it up before there was a result. Turk had torn up some photo of Kylie's or something.

Sophie's started singing some Christmas carols from her slot. It's nice. She hasn't sung too much since her sentence got extended.

Hey, you'll like this one. This girl called Kyla was telling me how she went to Med Unit yesterday with flu and congestion and stuff. So the sister put some Vicks in a bowl, put a towel over Kyla's head and had her inhale the fumes. But after a minute or two Kyla chundered, right in the bowl. Sister was burned off, but she changed the bowl, put more Vicks in, put the towel back on. A couple of minutes later Kyla chundered into it again. So this time, Sister made her keep the towel over her head and inhale the fumes from the Vicks and the vomit. Nice mixture, hey? Made her feel a whole lot better.

Anita just yelled out 'Anyone know the post-code for Breton?' 'Yeah' someone yelled back, 'S.U.X.'

You gotta laugh.

Keep singing Soph.

See you, Manna. Hope your Christmas was good. But what you said about Steve, I'd be worried. He sounds like he's blown his cork. Hope you get the post office job — at least you'll be away from him more.

Lotsa love,
Trace

≈

Dec 26, 3 a.m.

This letter's not over yet Manna. I just woke up with the worst dream: knives and bullets and blood, and shapes in the dark. Then I found I got my period — a rare event in here. Everyone dries up. So maybe that's why I had the dream. But I'm not going back to sleep — I don't want to go through that again. It was bad, a blood bath, bloody bad.

Sorry about the writing but I'm doing this by the light of the security lights outside my slot, with a bit of help from the moon. So it's not easy.

You know, Manna, I am going to try to change. Hell, I've changed a lot already, I think. But I'm going to get out of Maximum S. By the time I leave Macquarie you'll be proud to know me. I'll be the first woman Pope. Seriously though, I am going to have a go at it. A Block's for losers. But you got to help me, OK? Let me know when I'm being a bigger dickhead than usual. I've been on the street so long, I think it's normal to spit in the gutter. I forget how you're meant to act. But I'm gonna make it Manna, I really am.

'Night again,
                    T.

≈

                                        Dec 31

Dear Manna,

New Year's Eve — another thriller in downtown Garrett. It's party time again, with lights out at 9.30. I'm almost weak with excitement.

You said you had that party for Rebecca tonight. Hope it goes well. It's funny how you can fight with someone and hate their guts at times, but they get like a habit, and you miss them when they go. People are always leaving here.

The last time I went to a New Year's Eve party was at Buckley's Beach, two years back. Jeez it was a mess. People drinking and fighting and spewing everywhere. On the beach you were up to your ankles in condoms. The pigs came round every few minutes but they didn't try anything till about two o'clock, when everyone was too wasted to get them, so they had it all their own way. They sure spilt some blood — they had themselves a happy New Year. Raz and I got smart for once and melted into the night. Wise-ass Tracey, that's me.

We've got these workshop things going at the moment. I think because they're scared we'll get bored and chew the place down. So you can do drama or dance or meditation, all that kind of stuff. I'm doing writing. There's only three of us doing it, so you sort of have to go — you'd feel bad if you didn't. The lady who takes it is quiet but she's nice. She's had three books published but I haven't heard of her. Mary Lim, her name is. Do you know her? I told her about winning the prize for my story and she got quite excited about that.

We do these exercises like describing how a piece of chocolate smells, feels, looks and tastes. I liked that one — in fact I could do it over and over. And we did one where we had to exaggerate everything in a story. They're quite good. And she seems to like what I write. But the last workshop's on Thursday, bit of a bummer. I'm going to see if the library's got any of her books.

Well, I gotta go. You must owe me a few letters by now — you're getting slack. Guess the mail gets stuffed over Christmas and New Year. Tell Katrina to sort faster.

Oh yeah, I nearly forgot. Happy New Year!

Love,
    Trace

≈

Dear Manna,

Geez Manna where's all the letters? I haven't heard from you since Christmas Eve. Get your ass out of gear. Hope you're not sick or anything.

Things are starting to drag here. The workshops finished last week, and there's not much coming up that I know of. The hacks are so raggy. Roll call this morning was a good one — Mrs Neumann was doing it. When she got to Jenelle Hawthorne, Jenelle just answered 'Yeah', instead of 'Present'. Mrs Neumann snapped. 'Right, you're charged: attempting to escape.' 'What?' said Jenelle. 'Yes,' said Mrs Neumann, frothing at the mouth. 'You didn't answer your name correctly, therefore you're not here. And if you're not here, you must be in Med Unit or attempting to escape.' Can you believe it? I don't think she'll charge her though — she'd never get away with it.

I miss the basketball. Don't know if I told you, but we got chucked out for rough play and swearing and all that stuff. I don't know what they expected. I think they didn't like us winning so many matches.

Right now I'm sitting in the exercise yard, writing this. It's a nice day. There's a game of netball on — there's rings at both ends of the yard and a few lines on the ground. I'll go and play in a sec. There's not much else to do.

Hope there's a letter from you tomorrow.

See you,
        love,
                Trace

                    ≈

                        Jan 14

Dear Manna, three weeks since I had a letter from you and I'm getting worried. I suppose I'm scared that when I told you about my father, it might have, sort of, put you off. But you knew I was no angel. And anyhow, I don't think you're the kind of person to be put off that easily.

I'm worried about other things too. I'm still having these terrible dreams, horrible ones, full of people attacking each other. I wake up sweating and panting, and I'm scared to go back to sleep. So I don't sleep much.

I suppose what I'm saying is maybe these dreams make me worry about you, with your brother getting so ugly and all.

Anyhow, it's probably nothing — you've probably got flu or gone on holidays. And there'll probably be a letter tomorrow.

We had this theatre group came today, did a play called *Diary of Anne Frank*. It was good. I'm going to read the book.

Well, look forward to hearing from you, hopefully tomorrow.

Lots of love,
        Tracey ≈

Dear Manna,

Well, the end of the week and still nothing. I'll have to wait till Monday now.

It's funny, remember how I stopped writing to you when you got onto me for not being at Prescott High? And you were writing practically every day, trying to bully me into answering? And now the boot's on the other foot. Maybe I'd better start writing every day. I'll send you postcards that other people can read. Remember that? They put the mail on the board here and if you're five minutes late from classes your postcards get read by everyone in the place.

They're having a game of badminton at the moment. It's not a bad game, but I'm not in the mood. I'm just sitting in the corner watching now.

Have a good weekend Manna,

Love,
Tracey

≈

Dear Manna,

The mail's been put up, and right now I feel pretty terrible.

Manna, the second worst thing in the world would be if you decided to stop writing to me.

But the worst thing would be if anything bad happened to you. I don't know if I could stand it if you didn't want to write any more, but I know I couldn't stand it if you'd had an accident, or something. The most important thing right now is that you're OK. That's more important than if you hate me or despise me. What I'm saying is, if you're well and healthy, but you don't want to write, at least send me one sentence saying that. And then I guess I'll have to stop hassling you.

The hardest thing is not knowing. And being in here, I'm totally cut off. There's no way I can find out if you're OK. That's what's driving me crazy.

Please God, if you're there, let there be a letter tomorrow. And if there is, I'll be the best damn Girl Guide in this whole dump. Please write, Manna.

Luv ya,
Trace

≈

Jan 22

Nothing. What are you doing to me Manna? Why'd you write in the first place? Why didn't you leave me alone, like I told you? You've really screwed me up now, just when I was starting to get somewhere. I'm so scared Manna. Where are you?

≈

Dear Manna,

Well, now I know that something's wrong. I got six letters back today, all marked 'Return to Sender'. And it wasn't in your writing. They go right back to before Christmas. So all this time I've been writing into nothing, writing to myself.

There's nothing I can do Manna. I don't think I'm going to hear from you again. I hope that you're OK, but somehow I don't think you are. God bless you Manna — I still love you.

Your friend
Trace

≈

Feb 11

Dear Mandy,

I thought I'd write to you one last time. It's a year today since you sat down and answered my ad, on a rainy Sunday when you were bored. I've still got every letter you wrote, even though you're not meant to keep them, but I don't read them any more.

My last four letters came back too, as this one will if I bother to send it.

Manna, I'm sorry, but I'm not doing so well. I hope you're not disappointed in me. I've been in Med Unit for a while now, two or three weeks maybe. I don't do much, or say much. I like just sitting under my bed, watching things. But they're nice to me in here.

I still get the dreams though.

They say I won't be going back to A Block. I get the shakes when I think about it. I don't know where they'll send me. I hope, wherever it is, they'll be nice to me. I'd like to stay here but I don't think I'm allowed.

All I want is people to be nice to me.

Bye, Manna. Remember, just keep on goin' till it all stops flowin', OK?

Luv ya,
Tracey